"Matt, You Gave Up All Rights To Me The Day You Walked Out On Me."

"I know." He turned to face her, and Libby winced again at the pain in his eyes. "Or at least part of me does. The other part won't let me even admit that we're through. It keeps telling me…"

"Telling you what?" she asked softly.

"That maybe it isn't too late. That I can find out what it is you need to be happy."

"And when you do?"

"I'll give it to you." His voice was flat with certainty. "Whatever it is, whatever it takes."

Dear Reader:

Welcome to Silhouette Desire—provocative, compelling, contemporary love stories written by and for today's woman. These are stories to treasure.

Each and every Silhouette Desire is a wonderful romance in which the emotional and the sensual go hand in hand. When you open a Desire, you enter a whole new world— a world that has, naturally, a perfect hero just waiting to whisk you away! A Silhouette Desire can be light-hearted or serious, but it will always be satisfying.

We hope you enjoy this Desire today—and will go on to enjoy many more.

Please write to us:

Jane Nicholls
Silhouette Books
PO Box 236
Thornton Road
Croydon
Surrey
CR9 3RU

Husband Material

RITA RAINVILLE

SILHOUETTE
Desire

*First published in Great Britain 1996
by Silhouette Books, Eton House, 18-24 Paradise Road,
Richmond, Surrey TW9 1SR*

ISBN 0 373 05984 1

22-9607

Made and printed in Great Britain

RITA RAINVILLE

has been a favourite with romance readers since the publication of her first book. Rita has always been in love with books—especially romances. In fact, because reading has always been such an important part of her life, she has become a literacy volunteer and now teaches reading to those who have yet to discover the pleasure of a good book.

Other Silhouette Books by Rita Rainville

Silhouette Desire

A Touch of Class
Paid in Full
High Spirits
Tumbleweed and Gibraltar
Hot Property
Bedazzled

Silhouette Christmas Stories 1992
"Lights Out!"

To Joanne Fitzpatrick, Evelyn Seranne
and Patricia Vandivort...
good friends and a fine support group.

One

"**W**ell, hell."

Matthew Flint lowered the window of his large black Blazer, and looked across the street at the Gothic-style mansion that seemed to swallow half the block. A stark, unrelieved-gray monstrosity with turrets and towers looming high above the street, it looked down through shadowy mullioned windows at the other large but less pretentious homes in the quiet San Diego cul-de-sac. Surly-looking gargoyles, perched in niches on the angled roof, offered about as much welcome as a pair of sleek, lethal Dobermans.

Damn, it was even worse than he'd expected.

The house was a regal curiosity—one to which the reporters in the sunny city frequently paid homage. Their interest seemed to be divided equally between the owner—an eccentric inventor—and the structure itself.

It was also a security nightmare. Matt had known that much a year earlier when he'd glanced at the pictures accompanying an article in a local newspaper. At that time, his only reaction had been one of relief that in his business of corporate troubleshooting he rarely became involved in home security. But that had been then.

This was now.

It seemed natural for an eccentric inventor to live in a spooky mansion. Strange people often inhabited bizarre places, and according to newspaper accounts, Eli Trueblood was as strange as they came. So it was just fine—for him.

It was a whole different can of worms when the person staying there was Libby Cassidy. Small and utterly feminine, Libby had the heart of an Amazon but possessed not one shred of instinct for self-preservation. The first time Matt had seen her, he'd known that come hell or high water she was going to be his—in every way. And he'd been right.

Libby, his . . . lover.

Ex-lover, he thought in pained self-disgust as he got out and slammed the Blazer's door before stalking across the street. She had been an ex for exactly six months and three days—if anyone was counting. Anyone besides Matt Flint.

He didn't kid himself. If Matt was anything, he was a realist. No one else gave a damn. The only other person who had ever cared had been Libby, and he had changed that with a few words, tossed them at her as she'd come in from work, swinging through the door, an eager smile on her face.

It's been nice, sweetheart. Real nice. But I have a new job out of state, and since there's nothing to keep me here, I'm leaving.

He winced as he had every day of the past six months and three days, recalling the blossoming pain in her green eyes, the shaky breath she'd drawn and the proud tilt of her chin. Her coppery hair had swirled around her shoulders as she'd turned and walked silently back out the door, taking the sunlight with her.

Yeah, he'd been a real bastard, all right.

Intentionally.

He hadn't believed his luck when she'd agreed to live with him—or rather, to have him live with her, since he had moved into her white frame house on the pleasant, sleepy street. It was a dream come true—a woman who smiled at him when he came through the door, and when he unexpectedly caught her gaze all he saw gleaming in her jade eyes was love.

His time with Libby had been all that a man could hope for, but he'd known right from the start that she was a home-and-hearth type and figured their time together was temporary at best. He had been told often enough that he couldn't carry off a permanent relationship to believe it. Hell, all he had to do was look back over his life to see the truth of the matter. So he'd assumed that when she was ready to settle down, she'd look for another type of man—one who could keep her happy for the rest of her life. When the time came, he promised himself to get out of her life, grateful for what he'd had and leaving her with no guilt for kicking him out .

Their time together lasted longer than he'd expected, but not as long as he'd hoped. And when the time came to leave, it felt as if his heart had been torn out of his chest. But he'd kept his promise. As soon as he'd seen signs that she was interested in another man, he'd made the break fast and brutal so she wouldn't waste any time wondering how to tell him it was over. He'd rather have her mad as hell than hurting.

Yeah, he'd been a real charmer, all right.

And real smart, to deliberately get rid of the one woman in the world who could chase away the darkness. Who made him believe in the possibilities that most men took for granted. No doubt about it, he decided as he gazed at the huge double doors. She'd be real thrilled to have him back.

Libby Cassidy's slim fingers stilled on the computer keys as a deep, mournful gong reverberated through the house. The doorbell, she decided after a moment. Or the crack of doom. It was the first time it had rung in her twenty-four hours of residence. Apparently, Eli Trueblood didn't welcome impromptu visits and had trained his neighbors accordingly. The bell was as spooky as everything else in the enormous place, she mused as she pushed her chair back from the desk and stepped out of her temporary office. Her large, two-year-old golden retriever skidded around the corner to join her, nails clacking on the polished wooden floor as he whuffed a greeting.

"Come on, Sam," Libby encouraged, shivering when her voice echoed down the long hall. "Let's see who it is." The dog gave her a goofy grin and pranced beside her toward the front door.

House-sitting was not supposed to be an exercise in courage, Libby thought with another shiver as she hurried past a tarnished, grim-visaged suit of armor, flicking her finger against the front of its helmet to show that she wasn't intimidated. House-sitting was supposed to be pleasant, undemanding. She should know—it said so in the employment brochure she had written. And the fact that she and Carla had several dozen retired couples clamoring for the pleasant jobs proved the point, she reminded herself.

Of course, the clamor had faded to total silence as, one by one, the available sitters had taken a quick, aghast look at Eli Trueblood's Gothic horror and begun shaking their heads from side to side, muttering about prior commitments. Whatever comments had been made, "no" had been the unanimous response.

"Which is exactly what I would have said if I hadn't been a partner in the business," Libby assured Sam, giving him an absent pat. But business owners—especially those determined to come out on top—did a lot of things they didn't necessarily want to do, up to and including personally sitting San Diego's answer to Hollywood's spookiest haunted house.

Libby reached the massive double doors just as another gloomy peal tolled through the vast halls. "Of course, Eli wouldn't have anything as mundane as a peephole," she mumbled disgustedly, staring at the solid slabs of oak with misgivings. After the night she'd spent, she wouldn't be surprised if a werewolf stood waiting on the other side, gore dripping from his fangs.

She dropped her gaze from the solid doors to Sam. His head was tilted expectantly, his plumy tail wagging. "Okay," Libby warned, "I'll open it. But if it's someone named Igor, he's all yours."

She released the dead bolt and tugged at the heavy door, winced when the hinges gave a dismal groan and made a mental note to have them oiled. If Eli didn't approve, tough. Sam gave an impatient whuff, stuck his nose through the widening crack and wriggled through. Libby heard his delighted yelp before the door was fully open. "Sam, for heaven's sake, hold on. I'm right behind—"

Libby came to a dead stop, unable to utter a word, to move. Or breathe. She watched numbly as Sam danced on his hind legs, his front paws splayed on Matthew Flint's chest, his pink tongue making frantic attempts to lick the clean-shaven chin.

She had forgotten what a big man Matt was, that against his six-feet-three-inch frame, the top of her head barely reached his chin. Unfortunately, the rest of her memories were painfully clear. He was still dangerously lean, broad shouldered and slim hipped. His dark, coffee-colored hair was still thick, controlled by a severe cut, his chin just as stubborn. He was still clean shaven except for the mustache that her fingertips had once smoothed and teased. His cool gray eyes gazed at her with the same lack of expression they'd held on the first day she'd seen him—and the last.

Matt. The man to whom she'd given her heart and soul.

Matthew Flint. The man who, when he was through with them, had carelessly tossed them back.

"Hello, Libby."

"Flint." Libby gave him a brief nod. Keeping her voice level was a victory she didn't intend to reveal. The memory of six months of heartache and hard work helped bolster her courage, but she still clutched the doorknob, pulling the door closer until she was framed in a shaft of late-May sunlight. When his eyes narrowed, she knew he'd caught the significance of the single word.

Flint.

Not Matt.

Matt was the man she had loved, leaned against when she was helpless with laughter. The man she'd clung to, naked, cried out to in the dark nights. Flint was the businessman, as hard as nails and as sensitive as a tower of granite.

No, not Matt. Never again Matt.

Libby's brows rose as she took in the his pale blue knit shirt that stretched tautly across his shoulders and the faded jeans that did the same over his thighs. Those two items, along with his white running shoes, made a definite statement: he had not just left work—wherever that was these days. His theory was that the corporate world judged its employees by their clothes as well as their ability, so when Matthew Flint was on the job, he met the executives on their own turf with dark, costly suits and gleaming Italian shoes.

Libby's gaze dropped to Sam, who was now on all fours, looking as if he'd have to be surgically removed from his hero's leg. "Come on, Sam," she commanded softly. "It's time to go in." She opened the door wider and waited for the dog to move. When he didn't, her voice sharpened. "Sam, *now*."

The dog cast a pathetic look at the man beside him and trudged through the opening. As soon as his tail was clear, Libby said, "Goodbye, Flint," and pushed at the door. It didn't slam, which would have been satisfying. Instead, it swung ponderously and stopped a few inches from the jamb. Instinctively looking down, Libby wasn't surprised to see Flint's size-eleven shoe planted in the way.

Living with Matthew Flint for five months had been an education in several ways, Libby reflected wryly, staring at the white shoe. One thing she had learned was that when he wanted something, he didn't give up until he got it, and right now, apparently what he wanted was *in*. Well, that was just too damn bad, she decided angrily, flinging herself forward. With grim determination, she pressed her back against the door and dug the heels of her sandals into the Oriental carpet covering the entryway. His wants weren't real high on her list of priorities anymore. In fact, they had slipped right down off the bottom of the page.

Seconds later, she realized it was no contest. Slowly and inexorably, her feet were pleating the colorful carpet, sliding it across the oak floor before her as Flint's steady pressure pushed the door open. Before she was squashed into the wall, she jumped aside and spun around, fists on her hips, glaring at him. He stepped in and quietly closed the door behind him.

"Sam?" When the dog's cool nose touched her fingers, Libby said calmly, "Bite him."

Matt snapped his fingers and Sam lunged forward to lick the back of his hand. "He won't, you know. He remembers me too well."

And so do I, Libby thought with a shaky breath, almost undone by the dark, deep rumble of his voice as she tried to banish the memories swamping her.

So do I.

Memories of Matt—Flint, she corrected silently—his gray eyes gleaming with desire, his fingers stroking, gliding, caressing until she'd cried out, until she'd wrapped her legs around him, holding him so close he was a part of her. His pleasure in their quiet life, his contentment as long as they were together. And finally, a searing memory of him packing, calmly telling her he was leaving—leaving because there was no reason to stay.

"Okay." Libby stepped back, increasing the space between them. "You've proven you're stronger than I am. Now what?" She shrugged and lifted her hands in a gesture of annoyed exasperation, grateful that annoyance was the only emotion the movement revealed. Grateful that a six-month collection of hurt and anger wasn't included. Pride might be an overrated quality, she reflected grimly, but right now it was all that stood between her and a torrent of words that would reveal exactly how deeply she had been wounded. Pride didn't heal or offer warmth in a cold, empty bed—or life—but it was what she had left.

She gave Flint a quick, assessing glance, wondering what had brought him back. *Wondering?* she thought wryly, considering the lukewarm word. She'd give a year's income to know—but she wouldn't ask. Pride again. Coming back was the last thing she would have expected from Matthew Flint but then, what did she know? Six months earlier, if anyone had asked, she'd have sworn they had something special, something that neither of them would walk away from.

In her mind, they had been a couple, committed to each other with the same ties and loyalties that bound a married couple. She'd been wrong, and a mistake of that magnitude tended to leave a lasting impression. In her case, she figured she'd been lucky. There'd been no irreparable damage and she had learned a valuable lesson. The situation had taught her the dangers of trusting too easily and completely, and never, ever, to be so gullible again. She'd spent more time than she cared to count trying to convince herself it had been a fair exchange.

"All right," Libby said with a sharp sigh, "let's get this over with so you can leave, and I can get back to work. What do you want?"

You. "To talk." He shouldered his way around her and ambled down the hall, stopping to gaze thoughtfully at the suit of armor. He moved like a large, predatory cat. He always had. More memories, Libby admitted, hastily looking away from his snug jeans and lean hips. He would still be turning women's heads when he was ninety. She blinked, stunned when he added, "Actually, I'm here to help you pack and get out of this rabbit warren."

Libby opened her mouth and closed it with a snap. "Pack?" she finally managed.

"Yeah. You know, throw stuff in a suitcase and walk out the door?" Still concentrating on the armor, he ran a lean, tan finger down the breastplate.

"Walk... out the door?" Libby stared at him in disbelief. "Just like that?"

"Yeah, just like that."

Matt's gaze took in everything except the woman behind him. One quick, starved glance was all he had allowed himself, but it had been enough. He had seen her astonishment dissolve into acute wariness. He didn't want to see the pain. Once, he had witnessed—hell, had been the *cause* of—her jade eyes dulling with anguish, and that had been enough for a lifetime. But now he had her attention and he'd better talk while he had the chance.

"This is the way I see it." Matt winced before turning to face her. He was blowing it. His casual tone wouldn't fool anyone—except possibly a woman too furious to see beyond her own hurt. "We have two choices here. You leave, or I stay and provide protection in this godforsaken place."

"*We?*" Libby took a steadying breath. "Where do you get *we?* I've been on my own for quite a while now, remember?" Her eyes shot pure green fire at him. "I honestly don't believe this, Flint. You take off for God knows where, come back without a hello or how-have-you-been and expect me to walk away from my job? You're not just impossible, you're rock stupid!"

Fury colored every word and some of Matt's tension eased. He could deal with anger. Hell, he welcomed it. Libby's temper was as spectacular as her shimmering red hair, and he had missed it almost as much as he'd missed her. She couldn't run him off with anger. He could handle it—hell, he could handle anything except the lost look he'd last seen in her eyes.

"This place is too damn big," he said abruptly, turning to face her.

"So?"

"It's not safe."

"For who?"

"For you."

Even the soft fringe of her lashes didn't soften the temper glittering in her narrowed eyes. "Ah. For me. How considerate of you. You came all the way from—" She broke off abruptly, remembering she had no idea where he'd been.

"Phoenix."

"All the way from Phoenix to give me a hand. Thank you. Very much. But it wasn't necessary. I can't afford your kind of help."

Her words chipped at him with all the warmth of icicles, and Matt flinched, knowing he was getting exactly what he deserved—and that things were only going to get worse. He was right, and it didn't take any longer than the time it took her to draw a deep breath.

"You're just as high-handed as ever, aren't you, Flint? Well, you could have saved yourself the trouble and sent a telegram."

"It wouldn't have convinced you."

"Neither will you," Libby assured him. "I don't know why I'm bothering, but I'll tell you something. In the last six months—without you around—I've accomplished a lot. I quit a job that was going nowhere, and Carla and I started our own business. Sitting Pretty, a house-sitting service. The business is doing fine, and *I'm* doing fine, thank you. I've learned to cut through red tape and we've made quite a name for ourselves. We have over thirty couples working for us and we still don't have enough to handle our volume. And, somehow, it all got done without you."

Matt shoved his hands into his back pockets to keep them off her and out of trouble. She wasn't telling him anything he didn't already know. He may have been gone, but keeping track of her had probably preserved his sanity. With his ability to dig into certain computer files, and his contacts, he undoubtedly knew as much about her business—and the rest of her life—as she did. She and Carla Withers had recently been the subject of a newspaper article in the *Los Angeles Times* about young, successful Southern California entrepreneurs. The column had almost doubled their list of clients and they were still scrambling for more sitters.

Yeah, she had done a hell of a job for herself.

She had made sound business decisions—except for this latest one...staying in a house that was an open invitation to burglars and probably littered with booby traps. He took a deep breath and tuned back into her litany. She wasn't through yet, not by a long shot.

"We?" she asked again, tilting her head and giving him a level look. "No. I don't think so. You went away and I managed on my own. I'm still managing and I'll keep on managing. On my own. I don't need you or anyone else to protect me. Anyway, Eli Trueblood has his own built-in protection in the house. It's effective, if unique. Besides, you have a business to run, remember?"

"I'm on vacation," he said blandly, looking into the large room off the hall. In any other house it would be a living room. God only knew what the weird inventor called it. The room was enormous. Deep, old-fashioned walnut decorative molding bordered the ceiling, and its ragtag collection of chairs, sofas and tables were overwhelmed by potted plants growing in messy profusion.

"Vacation? How nice for you." Her voice was cool and she didn't give an inch. "Have fun." She reached back, opened the door and stood with her hand on the knob, waiting for him to leave.

Matt ignored the gesture. Instead, for the first time since she'd opened the door, his gray gaze met hers. His stomach clenched when he saw remnants of the anger and hurt she was trying to conceal. Taking a closer look, he felt his nerves tighten at the suspicion radiating from her expressive face and stiff spine. She didn't trust him and she made no attempt to hide the fact. Knowing that he deserved every bit of her skepticism didn't help.

The frustration in her eyes told him she'd like nothing better than to toss him out on his ear. He deserved that, too. But going through the door alone wouldn't solve the problem of her safety. He had a bad feeling about the house, had had it in Phoenix as soon as he learned she was staying here for a month. What he needed to do was get her safely back to her place, the peaceful white cottage with its worn porch swing and haphazard borders of bright flowers. Barring that, he was going to stay. Either way, he decided grimly, it was going to be an all-out battle.

Stalling so he could try a more oblique approach, he glanced around and asked, "Where's Dr. Frankenstein's laboratory?"

Libby blinked. "What?"

"There has to be one in a place this size," he added, wandering farther into the living room.

Accepting defeat for the moment, she shoved the door closed and trotted down the hallway, following him into the living room, determination in every step. Sam pranced at her heels. "Eli has a couple of rooms that look like workshops," she said briskly. "Look, Flint—"

"What the hell?"

Matt's soft oath cut her short and Libby's apprehensive gaze followed his across the room and settled on Sam. The dog had stalked to within three feet of the far wall and stopped, stiff legged, staring straight ahead at nothing. His hackles lifted and a growl rumbled deep in his chest. His lips curled back in a silent snarl.

"What's he doing?" Matt demanded.

Libby cleared her throat. "Growling."

"Hell, a blind man could tell that. What's he growling *at?*"

"I don't know. The wall. The bookcase." She shrugged. "He did it yesterday, too." Several times. Quivering with awful tension, just staring at the wall and baring his teeth. And each time, it had scared the wits out of her.

"Let's try this one more time, Libby," Matt said softly. "Are you going to be sensible and go home?"

Her gaze still on the quietly snarling dog, Libby shivered, grateful Flint had no idea how much she wanted to do exactly that. This wasn't just a big, old house. It was a *scary,* big, old house, and with Sam doing this hair-raising stuff, she was ready to run screaming out the door. "It's not that simple," she said slowly. "We have a contract with Eli and have to honor it."

"Why you?"

Libby sighed. "Kismet. Fate. Luck. Take your pick."

"Why you?" he repeated, not amused.

"Because Carla and I tossed a coin and I lost."

"That's a rotten reason."

She shrugged. "That's as good as it gets. Our business is small potatoes compared to some of the other house-sitting companies here in town, and word-of-mouth referrals have helped put us in the black. People recommend Sitting Pretty because we're dependable. We do exactly what we promise we're going to do. We *have* to. We can't afford the bad publicity we'd get if we backed out of this job."

"Are you saying that people would expect you—"

"To take care of their homes," she said flatly. "It would be the kiss of death to do anything else."

"So you're staying?"

She swallowed. "I'm staying."

Matt turned his scowling gaze from her to the stiff-legged Sam and back to her again. "All right, fine. If you're too stubborn to leave, you damn well won't stay here alone. The way I figure it, I owe you. You gave me a lot those months we were together. This will make us even. I'm going out to the Blazer for my gear. And Libby," he warned softly, "if you lock the door behind me, I'll kick the damn thing in."

Dazed, but knowing he meant exactly what he said, Libby watched him stalk down the hall and out the front door. She should be arguing, telling him to go to hell, not feeling limp with relief that she wouldn't have to spend another night alone in Eli's house. She should tell him to get lost, do the same kind of disappearing act he'd done six months earlier. Pride alone demanded that, she reminded herself. But with Sam all but tap-dancing and shouting, "Looky, a ghost!" she wasn't about to.

For a very simple reason—because just as pride wouldn't warm an empty bed, neither would it save a business. So if something weird, or worse, was going on in the house, she would need reinforcements. Unfortunately, she couldn't think of anyone more capable of handling trouble than a troubleshooter, and Flint was the best there was.

So what if he'd scraped her heart raw when he'd left? That was in the past, over and done with. Taking a deep, bolstering breath, Libby decided she wouldn't argue with him...for now. After twenty-four hours in Eli True-blood's house of horrors, she was already counting the days until she could leave. Proud she may be, but she wasn't stupid.

Flint's pragmatic, muscular presence could just save the day, and her business. If he wanted to play bodyguard and wasn't planning to charge outrageous corporate fees, he was welcome to prowl the house and deal with Eli's eccentric security system. And she could... Libby took a steadying breath. Heck, she assured herself, she could hold her breath for thirty days if it would help save the business.

As abruptly as he had frozen in position, Sam relaxed and turned to her with the canine equivalent of a shrug. He nuzzled her cold hand and followed when she backed up and collapsed into a stuffed chair. Libby ran her hand over his smooth head, taking as much comfort as she gave. "So your hero's back, huh, guy? How does he figure he owes me? And how do you suppose he knew where we were?"

Libby's hand stilled. That was a very good question. How *had* he known? Moving into Eli's house had been a sudden back-to-the-wall decision, and the move had been made just yesterday afternoon. Eli, who resembled a certain Mr. Einstein, and was probably just as focused, had absently agreed to her conditions, not realizing just how unusual they were.

Yes, he'd said, she could bring her dog—a situation absolutely forbidden by her own rules. Even though Carla had offered to keep Sam, Libby wasn't about to stay in the great racketing house by herself. Yes, she could set up her computer and run her part of the business from one of the small rooms. Yes, if necessary, she could be away from the house for more than the time specified by the contract. Yes, yes, she could do anything she wanted during her stay—he trusted her judgment, he'd said a bit testily. Once Eli had scrawled his initials on the amended contract, she had moved in, leaving Carla in charge of the office, which was nothing more than an empty bedroom in Libby's house.

Anyone looking for her, especially anyone who hadn't seen her for six months, would logically go to her house. Since she doubted that Carla would even open the door for Matthew Flint, how had he tracked her down? And why?

Libby shrugged. Flint had his ways. He'd told her more than once that people—especially the ordinary, law-abiding types—could always be found. As to the why, she'd eventually find out. Maybe. Of course, knowing Flint as she did, it was fairly safe to assume he had his own agenda, his own reasons for being here, and she could wonder till hell froze over, but she'd probably never know for certain unless he decided to tell her.

One thing she could be certain of—he hadn't returned to resurrect the past. He had been brutally clear about that when he'd left. *There's nothing to keep me here.* Well, nothing in that department had changed, she reflected stoically, so it stood to reason that whatever had brought him back didn't involve her. And whatever kept him here would be strictly business.

Two

Matt slammed the door of the Blazer, shouldered his duffel bag with a grim smile and headed back to the house before Libby could change her mind. He'd done it. He was in the house, and without a major battle. Of course, he was used to waging battles, both big and small, corporate and emotional, so it wouldn't have mattered. It was just easier this way.

Yeah, he'd had plenty of skirmishes over the years, and he'd started early, he reflected. As a youngster with older parents who were deeply involved in their careers and upwardly mobile life-style, he'd spent too many years vying for their attention. Finally, as a high school student, he'd decided that their abstraction had been a blessing in disguise. They had provided a roof over his head and food on the table, and he'd learned not to expect anything else, to go after what he wanted, to be accountable for his screwups and not to rely on anyone else for what he wanted. They had

been lessons that he had not forgotten and had undoubtedly contributed to his present success as a troubleshooter.
He now had a business he could base anywhere in the country, and he was his own boss.

The only time he had forgotten those lessons was when he
had married Caroline. He shook his head at the memory.
Talk about a disaster. Her parting shot after the divorce had
been that he didn't know how to love, he should never re-
marry and he didn't know how to keep a woman happy on
a long-term basis. Since her statement merely confirmed
what he'd suspected for a long time, he hadn't been too
surprised. He certainly hadn't been able to make *her* happy.
Of course, he thought with a philosophical shrug, she still
wasn't happy. And she called him up every now and then
just to let him know it was all his fault.

But that had been then. It was over and done with.

This was now.

He was back in the same house with Libby, and he could
thank Sam for that, not his own powers of persuasion. He
frowned as he took the porch stairs two at a time, thinking
about the scene that had turned the tide.

What was going on? Sam, the dog he'd always figured
would lick a burglar to death, had suddenly turned lethal.
If he'd found an intruder, he would have torn him apart.
And Libby? Her eyes had been huge and scared but she
would have jumped into the donnybrook right beside Sam,
with no more to protect her hide than a pink tank top,
matching shorts and flimsy thong sandals. She had the kind
of spirit and loyalty that was rare, the kind wise men
dreamed of finding in their mates, the kind he had dreamed
of finding. Hell, the kind he *had* found.

Yeah, once it had all been his. Until he'd loused up.

Big-time.

Matt closed the front door behind him, turning the dead bolt and testing the knob, wondering why he bothered. There were probably a hundred other ways to get into the place, all of them easier than fiddling with this sturdy bolt.

Libby poked her head out of the living room and stared at him. Apparently reassured, she stepped into the hallway, Sam at her side.

"Where do you want me?" he asked when she neared.

He had to give her credit. She didn't tell him, even though her expressive eyes listed hell as one option. He had news for her, he thought, following her silent progress down the hall. He'd been there—for six months and three days.

He roused himself from contemplation of her lush bottom long enough to note that the house looked as if a series of hyperactive contractors had been given full rein. It was a maze with halls going in all directions, some of them not seeming to lead anywhere. Stairways, spiral and straight, loomed up unexpectedly as they turned corners. When he counted the sixth, he wondered if Libby had been given a map along with the keys.

"This isn't a rooming house," Libby said abruptly, not even bothering to turn her head. "If I happen to cook, you're welcome to join me, otherwise you help yourself. I stocked food in the fridge and the cupboards. I'll be working in my office a good deal of the time, so if you make a mess, you'll have to clean up after yourself. That goes for your room, too."

"Libby?"

She finally stopped and pointed into a large, cluttered room with a huge bed. A man-size recliner, dresser, several tables, a variety of lamps and a stack of boxes against one wall completed the decor.

"This is yours. You'll have to live with the boxes. Almost every room has them. If being a pack rat was a crime, Eli would be serving a life sentence.

"I'm on the other side of the house," she explained in a rush. "You're welcome to wander around, get familiar with the place. Except for my room. It's off-limits." Still not looking at him, she added in a level voice, "But of course you don't need to be told that. After all, there's nothing for you there."

"Libby?"

She turned and started marching back the way she'd come.

"Libby, damn it, will you listen to me?"

She hesitated then turned to face him. "What?"

Now that he had her attention he didn't know what to say. That he had been a damned fool? That he had been waiting for an excuse to come back? That he'd give everything he had to see her green eyes filled with welcome instead of wariness? That he had come back for his woman—whether he deserved her or not? Sure, Flint, that's just what she's waiting to hear—that she's a real lucky lady. A genuine idiot is giving her another chance to be savaged. Matt closed his eyes and swore softly.

"Well?"

Challenge coupled with warning cooled her voice even more. Whatever her reason for letting him stay, it wasn't because she wanted him here. More than likely it was because she felt she was up that well-known creek without a paddle and thought he might have an extra oar. But she was also serving notice—they were on her turf, using her rules.

"It'll work out, you'll see." Matt winced at the sound of his voice. Rough edged and hard, it didn't exactly inspire confidence, and the few words he'd ground out weren't much better. If the expression on her face was any indication, Libby agreed with him.

"It better," she said bleakly, turning away. "My business is riding on it."

Her business.

Matt gazed after Libby until she turned down one of the hallways, leaving only the soft slapping sound of thong sandals hitting her heels at every brisk step. She wasn't exactly running, but she wasn't wasting any time getting away from him.

Looking at the situation from her point of view, he couldn't blame her. He had hurt her once and she wasn't hanging around for seconds. From his viewpoint, it was pure hell listening to the sound of her retreating footsteps, especially when he needed the feel of her against him as much as he needed his next breath.

Sighing sharply, he stepped into the bedroom, deliberately turning his mind to Libby's house-sitting enterprise. It was obviously her top priority and he couldn't blame her. It wasn't easy getting a small business off the ground these days.

Matt upended his duffel bag and dumped the contents on the bed. Stuffing underwear and socks in one drawer of the large, dark chest, jeans and T-shirts in another, he thought about Libby Cassidy and Carla Withers, entrepreneurs and cousins. They had come a long way in six months, and with their know-how, drive and sassy determination they'd end up at the top of the heap. Libby was a lot better off than she'd been at the advertising agency, banging her head against the glass ceiling, watching less qualified men get the promotions she'd deserved.

He was reaching for the last shirt when his hand closed around a slim, lethal knife clipped in its sheath. He gazed at it, absently testing its balance on his fingertips. It was an old friend, familiar and efficient—and always close at hand. He slid it beneath his pillow and straightened, automatically registering the exits in the room—two windows with flimsy locks and the door. Since they were entries, as well, he shook his head in disgust. Eli Trueblood might as well hang a welcome sign to burglars on the porch and be done with it.

Checking the room was instinctive, left over from days when it had been a necessity rather than a reflex, days spent working for the military, the government. It had been a job tainted by conflicting political policies and he'd gotten out as soon as he could. The years hadn't been a total waste, however. He'd learned enough questionable skills to anticipate the bad guys and become a top troubleshooter in the corporate world. They were extremely marketable skills and he had more work than he could handle these days. Even when he had moved to Phoenix six months ago so he wouldn't be running into Libby every time he turned around, people in trouble found him.

Now, the instinctive caution required no particular awareness on his part nor did it distract him from his immediate concern about Libby. In the general scope of things, her preoccupation with a growing business was small potatoes compared with what he could have found, he reflected with barely acknowledged relief. It could have been worse, a lot worse. There could have been another man hanging around.

Absently reaching down to grab the other pillow and toss it to the far side of the bed, Matt wondered why there *wasn't* one. There sure as hell had been one six months ago. So where was he? No man in his right mind would let his woman tackle a place like this alone. If he couldn't pry her away, he should be there with her.

Matt tossed the duffel bag beside the dresser and stretched out across the bed, yawning hugely. Folding his hands behind his head, he closed his eyes, considering a nap. For the past twenty-four hours, he'd been going nonstop. When he'd learned about Libby's temporary move to Trueblood's house of horrors, he'd spent several hours tying up loose ends and turning everything over to Jeff Morrison. For once, his second-in-command's poker face had failed him. It told Matt exactly what everyone on the staff thought about him—that he had become a robot, working sixteen to eighteen hours a day, seven days a week, that he no longer had a life outside the company.

He had delegated with a vengeance, leaving a pile of papers on his secretary's desk as high as the one on Jeff's and told them the business was their baby for the next few weeks. Then he'd climbed into the Blazer and headed for San Diego. A plane would have made it quicker but he'd opted to drive for two reasons—he wanted his own wheels and his knife.

His mind circled back to Libby and the presence, or lack, of another man. He had loomed large enough in her life six months earlier. Jason Trent, the new man in her department at the advertising firm. He was all she had talked about those last few weeks. So where was he now?

Matt ran his hand through his hair and sat up, swearing softly as he swung to his feet. Who was he kidding? He wasn't going to sleep. Not now. For the first time in six months he and Libby were under the same roof, and he needed her within reach more than he needed rest. A few answers wouldn't hurt, either.

After trekking down several dead-end hallways, he reached the main area and headed past the scruffy suit of armor, wondering idly what Eli Trueblood's lab looked like. Equipped better than the house, he assumed. Actually, the inventor was astute enough to keep the place in top-notch condition with working, modern conveniences. It was just the furniture that gave the illusion of shabbiness.

There were no expensive antiques, valuable artworks or knickknacks—at least not as far as he'd seen. In fact, it looked as if the inventor had hit every secondhand store in San Diego in an attempt to fill the rooms with furniture. There were large pieces to fit the massive, high-ceilinged rooms but nothing of intrinsic value.

Just as Matt heard the clicking of computer keys, Sam bounded up to give him an enthusiastic greeting. They met in the doorway of Libby's makeshift office, and Matt absently patted the dog's head as he looked around with appreciation. She already had her equipment up and working. After shoving several lounge chairs and tables into one corner, she still had room to accommodate the two worktables, one laden with her electronic equipment—computer, printer, modem, telephone and fax. Files and a vase of fresh yellow and white daisies graced the other.

When Libby looked up from the screen, her brows arching in a silent question, he studied her distant expression and swore silently, reading her reservations as clearly as if she'd written them on a sheet of paper and thrust it under his nose.

He'd do whatever it took. He'd have her back, he promised himself. Soon.

Damned soon.

Some of the tension left him when he realized she wasn't as composed as she wanted him to believe. His eyes narrowed in satisfaction when she scowled at him and continued typing. She was putting on a good show, he reflected, but it wasn't good enough to fool a pro. Finally, she snatched her fingers from the keys and folded her hands in her lap. Good. She was beginning to get rattled, and that's exactly how he wanted her. If he couldn't have her in his arms, he wanted her on edge and watching every move he made.

Matt propped a shoulder against the doorjamb and nodded toward her computer. "You didn't waste any time settling in, did you?"

Libby eyed him suspiciously, then said calmly enough, "I couldn't. I was swamped even before Eli called. I told him I'd have to set up an office here if I came."

"He didn't mind?"

"I don't even think he heard me. He's a funny old geezer, but I like him. He was so anxious to hare off to some conference he said I could do anything I wanted as long as I stayed." She shrugged and leaned back in her chair. "So here I am."

Matt watched her until she shifted uncomfortably and turned her attention back to the computer screen. "You look like an up-and-coming executive, even without a fancy desk." And she did. Even in hip-hugging, skimpy shorts, a matching top and a kissable mouth. She also looked good enough to eat.

"That's exactly what I am. A busy one," she added pointedly.

"What can I do to help?"

Libby tilted her head and gazed at him thoughtfully. "You mean it?"

Matt moved closer and settled a hip on the corner of the table nearest her, crowding her a bit. "I wouldn't have asked if I didn't."

He saw the flicker of memories in her green eyes and followed her thoughts as easily as if she had spoken them aloud—to the first time he'd told her he wanted her. He'd also told her that he'd be faithful. And honest. That he'd never lie to her. And he never had…until that last day when five words condemned him to a living hell for six months.

Nothing to keep me here.

"Hallelujah! I was hoping you'd say that." Libby broke the taut silence and hurriedly rolled her chair away from him. Snatching a cluttered file of papers, she handed them to Matt. "Eli left these with me, probably so I wouldn't get lost. They're the plans for the house. When I'm working, my usual procedure is to walk through the house every day, checking every room. And all around the outside," she added after a few seconds of thought. "Of course, in a normal house, it's a breeze. It only takes a few minutes. This place is different. It's—"

"A nightmare?"

"Unique," Libby finished tactfully.

"If you mean as in strange or weird, you're right."

Libby shrugged. "Whatever." Her brows lifted in an are-you-through expression.

"Go on."

"I'm trying to say it will save me a lot of time if you'll take over that part of the routine—time I need to use the phone and deal with these forms. This is the busiest season in this business and there are always people who wait until the last minute to plan their vacations, then expect miracles."

"And you provide the miracles?"

Libby gave a satisfied nod. "You betcha. If we do, they'll remember us the next time they leave town. So far, we've done pretty well. That's why business is booming."

Matt looked at the paperwork stacked in neat piles around her computer. "It looks to me as if you need a full-time secretary."

"Right again." Libby smiled complacently, touching a mound of contracts. "But now that we can afford one, we don't have the time for interviews. I'm too busy with the bookkeeping, and Carla's swamped at her end." She nodded toward the sheaf of papers in Matt's hand. "Are you sure you don't mind?"

Matt opened the file and flipped through several pages of blueprints. "What am I looking for?"

Libby shrugged, her fingers beginning to move over the keys. "Anything unusual. Make sure the plumbing hasn't sprung a leak, windows aren't broken, ceilings haven't caved in. That sort of stuff."

"Okay." He closed the folder and got to his feet. "I'll get started now."

"Uh..." She hesitated, giving him a quick, oblique glance, wondering again if she had lost her mind. Letting him stay with her had to be the worst idea of the century. She was asking for trouble. In spades. She also didn't have much choice, she reminded herself grimly. Her future was at stake here. Deciding to deal with the complexities later, she opted for simple gratitude. "Thanks."

Matt waited, motionless, until she finally turned toward him, her gaze wary. "You're very welcome, Libby. It's my pleasure."

She blinked. "You, uh, might want to take Sam along. He'd probably enjoy getting out of here for a while."

Matt shook his head. "Not now. I don't want you left alone while I'm outside or at the far end of the house. I'll call him when I get back here."

Libby opened her mouth to protest then closed it, knowing the last thing she wanted to do was argue the point. Although she might be banned from the staunch sisterhood of free and independent women for the thought, there was occasionally something to be said for macho, take-charge men.

"Whatever." She shrugged carelessly, hiding her relief. "I'll be here working if you need me for anything."

"I'll know where to find you, Libby," he said evenly as he moved toward the door. "I always will."

Libby blinked, listening to the blood roar through her veins and promised herself she wouldn't allow it to happen again. *It* meaning an involvement with Matthew Flint. She had learned a few things since her former boss and owner of the advertising agency had called Matt in to resolve some computer shenanigans. After a day of finding his steady gaze on her every time she looked up, of seeing the hunger in his gray eyes, she had gone out to dinner with him. They hadn't even finished their meal before he'd told her he wanted her. His words were as direct as his gaze, and she had been as vulnerable as a small fish with a shark on its tail. He had made her feel as no other man ever had—desirable, alluring and totally female. A week later, she was making room in her closets for his clothes.

For five months, she had been cherished in ways she thought only existed in movies and books. She had been teased, wanted and very thoroughly loved. No, she thought in instant denial, not loved. Love doesn't change in the blink of an eye. Face it, she told herself for the thousandth time. What they'd had was good sex. That's all it was. When it was over, he was gone, and she had learned a few things— mainly that a woman should never give her heart and soul to a man who only wanted a body.

Dismissing the memories but keeping the lesson firmly in mind, Libby cleared her throat, stopping him in the doorway. "Oh, by the way..."

"Hmm?" Matt looked back over his shoulder, the full force of his gray gaze on her face.

"Watch out for the peacocks."

"The what?"

Libby bit back a satisfied smile at his startled expression. Since it wasn't easy to disconcert the hotshot troubleshooter, she leaned back to savor the moment.

"Peacocks," she repeated with another small smile. "In the backyard. They tend to crowd people a bit. I think they're used to Eli feeding them and they get a little aggressive if you go out there without food."

"Terrific. What do they eat?"

"Well, I know they chomp on the fruit in the trees. Eli didn't leave any special feeding instructions. If they start crowding you, pick something off the nearest tree and toss it to them."

"Terrific," he said again, waiting, gazing at the coppery head bent near the screen. "Is there anything else I should know before I take off?"

Libby's fingers moved swiftly over the keys. "Like the rumors that the place is haunted?"

"Haunted houses I can handle," he muttered, stepping into the hall. "I'm not so sure about hungry peacocks."

Or women. Woman, he amended. Just one, half his size, who could still tie him in knots.

"No," he said firmly to the hopeful, cavorting dog. "You stay here."

Sam gazed longingly after Matt, then collapsed on the floor with a mournful groan.

Libby turned from the screen to look bleakly at the abandoned dog. "Don't get your hopes up," she advised, knowing she really wasn't talking to Sam. "He left once and he'll leave again…just as soon as he gets whatever he came for."

Midnight. The witching hour.

Too restless to sleep, Matt sprawled in the recliner he'd pulled near the open door of his dark room, listening to the settling house. The temperature had dropped from a balmy eighty degrees to sixty and the wood-framed house creaked in mild complaint, grumbling its litany from roofline to floor.

Closing his eyes, Matt considered Eli's house. Actually, two houses, he silently amended. Two rambling houses that had been turned into a single structure some fifty years earlier by simply adding a wide connecting corridor. Forty-two rooms, all in good repair. The corridor had later become a huge indoor pool. A pool that was in excellent condition and now had an adjoining, roomy hot tub. His mind drifted to Libby, picturing her in the pool, wrapped around him in the steaming tub.

Matt jerked his mind back to the house, with its two full floors and parts of a third, complete with a widow's walk and turrets jutting up in unexpected places—a perfect blend of Gothic and Victorian horror. And it didn't take a rocket scientist to realize that with an owner who walked around in a creative fog, it was also a great setting for monkey business. Someone smart enough could use the place for anything from a traveling crap game to drug drops... and Eli Trueblood wouldn't have a clue. Matt shifted restlessly. His instincts were chanting a song and the lyrics had only one word—trouble.

Wondering what one old man wanted with all the space, Matt gave an exasperated sigh. It had taken him two hours to prowl through the maze of rooms, checking the flimsy locks on the doors and windows and giving the fixtures in the bathrooms a cursory inspection. Eli apparently had a penchant for suits of armor. There had been a couple of them around the pool and at least one in every long hall, sometimes two or three. He'd lost count of them before he'd covered all the rooms.

Security was so pathetic a five-year-old could break in. And the yard, despite the screeching peacocks, wasn't much better. There was at least an acre of lawn and untrimmed bushes, bordered by a small white picket fence that Sam could step over without even scraping his stomach.

And no alarms.

Matt stiffened at a new sound in the hallway, then eased silently out of the chair and reached for his knife. He'd been expecting something, but not this soon, and not the measured tread of footsteps down the length of the wide hall. If it wasn't Libby—and it wasn't—then it was trouble. Whoever it was, was making no effort to muffle the sound or avoid the creaking planks. Whoever it was had more courage than caution and was dumb as dirt.

Easing to the door, he stood as silent as a shadow, flashlight ready in one hand, his knife gleaming darkly in the other. He waited until the dim figure passed, then slipped into the hallway, following, the sound of his footsteps drowned out by the other.

"All right, that's far enough. *Freeze.*" He turned on the blinding beam of the flashlight and aimed it at head level, moving closer. Matt stopped and blinked, his harsh order fading to a baffled question. "What the hell?"

The moving figure didn't flinch, turn or stop. Bathed in the shaft of light from Matt's flashlight, it continued striding down the center of the hall, raised hand clenching a thick club. Matt stayed where he was, swearing softly in surprise.

An animated suit of armor, for God's sake, carrying a mace. A robot. That was what he had tried ordering around. Fascinated, he followed at a leisurely pace, keeping a fair distance behind, recalling Libby's earlier cryptic comment. So this is what she'd meant about Eli's effective but unique security system. He grinned as he pictured the hunks of armor he'd passed earlier doing sentry duty in the other long halls.

Eli's ingenuity boggled the mind. No doubt about it, Matt reflected, the system *was* unique but its effectiveness was questionable. It might scare away nervous and inept intruders, but the cool ones would soon realize that danger was almost nonexistent and would simply carry on with what they were doing.

When the armor did an about-face at the end of the hall, Matt remained where he was until it returned and was close enough to touch. Matt stepped aside, biting back a surprised oath when the robot followed. It stepped forward until it touched him, nudging him back. He repeated the maneuver several times, with the same results.

Matt's brows shot up in silent appreciation. The system wasn't so benign after all. Whatever Eli Trueblood was, he was no slouch when it came to heat-seeking devices. Making a mental note to have a long discussion with the inventor, Matt found himself being nudged toward the wall. Curious to see how the robot would restrain him, he was obligingly backing up when an enraged shriek broke the silence of the house.

Libby.

Three

———

"**D**amn it, get *out* of here!" Libby shouted.

Matt stiff-armed the robot to a dead stop, ducked beneath the raised mace and tore down the dark hall. "Libby?" His roar was met with another furious yell from her, followed by an ominous thunk as something heavy hit a wall.

"I said *out!*"

Matt rounded the corner into the main hall at a flat out run, aware that her voice carried more anger than fear and that his personal nemesis was still following him. In addition, he had caught the interest of two other robots as he'd bolted through their territory. They'd fallen in behind the first one, maces high and threatening, their pace increasing with his.

A wrathful Libby stood in the hallway just outside her bedroom door, framed in a rectangle of light. Her hair was a tumbled cloud of copper and she was clutching several books that appeared to be thick, scholarly tomes. Her night wear was as seductive as ever, he noted, eyeing the purple, outsize T-shirt that hit her at midthigh.

"I'm tired of these midnight strolls," she snapped, glaring at a retreating robot as she heaved a book at him. "I didn't get any sleep last night, and enough is enough."

Matt upped his speed a notch. "Libby, get your butt in your room and close the door. *Now.*"

"Not until this hunk of tin goes away and stays away." She hefted another book and stepped away from the doorway to get a better shot.

"Don't follow it," Matt barked as he neared her, his heart steadying when he saw that she was safe. Furious, but safe. Still, it wasn't going to be easy keeping her that way, he calculated, risking another glance over his shoulder. Libby didn't seem in a cooperative mood and the three stooges behind him were closing in for the kill.

"Damn it, woman, *move.*" He scooped her up in his arms without breaking his stride and hauled her into her room, dropping the knife on the floor as he kicked the door shut behind them.

It wasn't a second too soon. The solid wood shuddered with the impact of three heavy robots smacking into the door. Sam cautiously poked his head up from behind the bed, took a long look at Matt and Libby, then slowly sank back down, apparently deciding he was no longer on duty.

Libby dropped the book she had been cradling in her arms and took a shaky breath, shifting her stunned gaze from Matt's face to the agitated thuds on the heavy door and back again.

Her hand tightened on his shoulder. "Is that what I think it is?"

Matt's arms tightened around her. It felt so good to hold her. So damn good. "Probably," he replied vaguely, his thumb stroking her arm.

"The robots?" When he nodded, she shifted in his arms, knowing she should tell him to put her down. In a second, she promised herself. Maybe a minute. Looking anywhere but directly at him, her gaze focused on the knife, its blade gleaming gold in the reflected light from the lamp. "You still carry that thing around?"

"Always."

His hair was still damp from a shower and his light blue cotton shirt was open down the front with the sleeves rolled to his forearms. He held her high against his bare chest, his crisp, dark hair brushing against her sensitized skin.

Libby swallowed. He was too close, too warm.

Too overwhelming.

And way too familiar.

She closed her eyes for a long moment as memories and yearning battered at her, conjuring up needs she had buried six months ago, needs she had believed long gone. Forgotten.

She had been wrong. Oh, God, so very wrong.

Matt's heat wrapped her in a cloak of warmth, and Libby laced her fingers together, clenching them until her knuckles whitened, suddenly terrified that she would reach out and touch him. That she would caress the hard, strong man who for five months had held her so possessively in his arms at night. That she would reveal what she hadn't even admitted to herself—body and soul, she still wanted Matthew Flint.

She jumped at another crash outside the door. "Good grief, they're going to rip the door off its hinges," she muttered, trying valiantly to ignore his nearness.

"Mmm." Matt nodded, brushing his thumb along the soft skin of her arm.

Libby felt the jolt of heat all the way to her heart. "Put me down." Her words were little more than a strangled whisper.

Matt took in her widened eyes, shadowy with apprehension, and instinctively tightened his arms around her. "Don't be afraid of me," he muttered. "Tell me to go to hell, use my knife on me, anything. For God's sake, just don't . . . be . . . afraid."

She wriggled and tried to put more conviction in her voice. "I'm not. I just want you to put me down."

"In a minute," he murmured.

She knew that tone, had heard it too many times to be mistaken. Soothing, focused, the voice of a hunter talking down his prey. Panic flared through Libby when she saw the sensual intent in his rain-colored eyes.

Squirming in earnest now, she scissored her legs, managing to clip him on the hip with her heel. Her voice sharpened. "Put me down, Matt. *Now.*"

Matt narrowed his eyes, taking his time. Finally, he eased Libby down the length of his body, so slowly she felt every breath he took, every lean, hard inch of him. Her breath caught in her throat when her thigh brushed against the growing hardness beneath his jeans.

It had always been that way, she remembered hazily when her toes finally touched the floor and she stepped back. He had always wanted her, always needed her, and never bothered to hide the fact. He might not have loved her but his need has been undeniable.

Deliberately wrapping old hurts around her like a protective blanket, Libby walked to the windows, putting more distance between them, recalling the day he had left. The *way* he had left. Crossing her arms beneath her breasts, she reflected that even though he was back, she didn't know for how long. Even worse, she still didn't know which part of their life together had been the truth, which part an illusion.

Libby stared for a long moment at the dark beyond the panes of glass, recalling the emptiness of the past six months. Finally, bringing herself back to the present, she said in an even voice, "We're going to have to do something about Eli's guards in the hallway. If we don't, we'll never get any sleep."

"You called me Matt just now." He didn't try to hide his satisfaction.

Libby closed her eyes in exasperation. Damn. One lousy slip of the tongue and she was never going to hear the end of it. As always, he had looked for a weakness—and found it. She cleared her throat. "And the big guys aren't the only ones out there," she persisted.

"Not Flint, Libby. You said Matt." He crossed to her side of the room.

Her voice grew louder. "Pretty soon, while the big ones are still roaming around, the whiz kids will come out." Libby's eyes widened in alarm as his reflection loomed up behind her. "They're cute little buggers," she said hurriedly. "Come up to about my waist. They scoot around so quietly you can't even hear them, but they have absolutely no sense of direction so they keep bumping into things. Makes a heck of a racket," she ended breathlessly, wondering if she had managed to divert him.

She hadn't.

He moved closer. "I'm not Flint to you, Libby. Flint is a hard-nosed bastard of a businessman who supposedly won't give his own mother a break." He curved his hands around her slim shoulders and drew her back against him. "But you're not business, and except for one second of unbelievable stupidity, I've never been that way with you. And you have my solemn promise that I never will be again."

Libby spun away from Matt, holding out a hand to stop him.

She should have known better, she thought a second later when his fingers closed around her wrist. It was like trying to stop a locomotive with a cobweb. She should never have let him in her room, she reflected, forgetting she hadn't had much choice in the matter. No, what she *should* have done was stop him at the front door—slamming and double-bolting it as soon as she'd seen him.

"Libby?"

She shook her head, never taking her gaze from his face. "No. I don't want to hear it."

"Hear what?"

"Whatever you're going to say."

"What if I say I'm sorry?"

"Then I'd say you should be," she told him promptly, yanking her hand out of his. "You *were* unbelievably stupid. I'd also say it's a little late to be sorry. No, make that a lot late."

Backing up a safe distance and perching on the wide windowsill, she shifted restlessly under his steady gray gaze. She was nervous, she realized with annoyance, resisting the urge to tug at the thigh-length T-shirt. She felt exposed, which was stupid. Her shirt was cotton and built to fit a linebacker, and there was nothing sexy or revealing about it. The only problem with it was the number of times she had worn it when she was with Matt—and he had taken it off that exact same number of times.

But that wasn't a problem. Those things were all in the past. They were over and done with. So there was nothing to be worried about.

Except, maybe, the determined expression on Matt's face.

It wasn't a good sign, Libby reflected, giving him another quick glance. He had something on his mind, and, as always, he wasn't going to leave until he'd had his say. Libby gave a heavy sigh. She was tired, in no mood for midnight discussions, and she had never enjoyed poking a finger into open wounds.

"All right," she said abruptly, tired of the cat-and-mouse game. "Why are you really here, Matt? What did you come for?"

His quick grin should have warned her.

It didn't.

His mustache twitched, kicking up in one corner when he smiled. "You're getting slow, Libby. Six months ago you would have had it figured out before I got through the door. I came for you."

I came for you.

Matt swore softly the next morning, thinking about his words as he finished his sentry go-round. It was the last thing he'd meant to say. At least, right then. His attention had been focused on that damned T-shirt, watching it slide down one of her satiny shoulders. He remembered the shirt—and the shoulder—well. It would be hard to forget, considering that he'd taken it off her more times than he could count. He also remembered what it covered—pert breasts that just fit his cupped hand, a slim waist, a triangle of soft red hair beneath the curve of her belly and a lush bottom.

Yeah, his attention had definitely been somewhere else, and today he was paying for it. Libby was avoiding him. She had already eaten by the time he'd gone to the kitchen for breakfast, and she'd made herself scarce ever since.

He shook his head in disgust. It was no wonder she was running. He had planned to ease back into her life, to prove how much she needed him, that she couldn't do without him. And in four words, he'd blown the whole thing. Now, assuming she didn't kick him out, he'd have to give her some more time to forget, or adjust to him being back, and try again. It would work. It had to. And he could wait. If he'd learned anything in his line of work, he'd learned to be patient. Besides, he owed her that much. She needed time to heal and, if he was real lucky, time to trust him again.

Sam pranced up and licked his hand, nudging him toward Libby's office. Matt stroked the dog's head. "Right. That's just where I was heading."

He stopped in the doorway and waited until she looked up from the computer screen. "Morning, Libby," he said with a small smile. A frown of concentration creased a vertical line between her eyes, and it only took one blink for wariness to replace the concentration. He tried to ignore it. "You'll be glad to know that the house is still intact. No broken windows, no bathtubs sinking through the floors. All's well in Trueblood Towers."

"Matt." She acknowledged him with a brief nod, her smile as cool as her eyes.

That one brief glance told him everything he needed to know. She was going to freeze him out, send him back to his frigid existence in one of the hottest cities in the country. *The hell she was.*

Fury and fear raced through him with the speed of a summer storm. He wanted to yank her up, haul her into his arms, toss her on the nearest bed and cover her with his body. But what he did was fold his arms across his chest, prop his shoulders against the doorjamb and smile. "Do we have a problem?" he asked softly.

Whatever she had geared herself up for, she changed her mind. He could see it in the shaky breath she took, the way her gaze skated past his. He took a long, deep breath himself.

"Nothing that a good night's sleep won't cure," she muttered, poking at her keyboard. "Did you have any trouble getting back to your room last night?"

Matt shrugged. "Not really. I skulked down the halls, peeking around corners. Your friend Eli is a certified genius, but it's not too hard to avoid his heat-seeking missiles if you give them plenty of room."

Libby shivered. "Better you than me. Those maces could crack someone's head like a dropped squash. And I was out there heaving books at one of them."

"Yeah, I thought about that last night while I was charging down the hall in front of them." He frowned at her averted face. "They're set up on a light sensor to start moving when the hall lights go out. It would be easy enough to disconnect the ones in this area if you want me to."

"I suppose we could leave the lights on." Her brows rose questioningly.

"We could, but Eli might have to choose between paying you and the electric bill."

Libby winced. "Forget it. Disconnect them. Please."

"Consider it done." When she gave a sigh of relief, he decided not to mention the new living arrangements that went with the promise. "I also checked out your cute little friends last night."

Libby looked up, directly at him this time. "The whiz kids?"

"Yep." His smile was amused. "They're amazing. I can't wait to meet your mad scientist."

"Not mine, thank God. But he's a very nice man." She gave a small shrug. "Weird, but nice."

"I'm serious. I like the way his mind works."

"You would." She reached for a file and turned to the computer. "Well, if you're still here at the end of the month, he'll—"

"I'll be here."

Libby's brows rose at the unmistakable edge to his voice. "No need to get testy," she said, checking the figures on the screen. "I was just—"

"I said I'll be here."

Oh boy. Libby briefly closed her eyes. It was going to be a long month. "Look, Matt, I don't know—"

"Matt," he repeated, satisfaction replacing the challenge in his voice.

"It *is* your name," she said reasonably, watching his eyes flicker as he tried to follow her logic. It wasn't difficult, she reflected disgustedly. Especially when all she was doing was trying to crawl out of a self-dug hole. Calling him *Flint* to make a point was one thing; trying to do it all the time was a lost cause, even though she'd planned to do exactly that. Last night had been a perfect example of habit taking over in a stressful moment. There was no way she'd be able to call him Flint for a month. Besides, the point had been well and truly made.

And received.

Matt sat on the corner of her desk, his long legs behind her chair. "Libby, about last night. I want to—"

She flung out her hand to stop him, remembering too late it was the same gesture she had made the night before. Matt took her wrist again, only this time he tugged, pulling her to her feet.

Drawn by his heated gaze, Libby moved closer, knowing she shouldn't, knowing she couldn't resist. The blood roared through her veins, almost drowning the little voice that warned her Matt was nothing but trouble. Almost, but not quite. He had hurt her once, it reminded her, and he'd hurt her again. Even as she agreed, her fingers touched his cheek, brushed his mustache, and she stepped closer yet, until she stood between his thighs.

One small part of her mind thought, *why not?* Just this once. One kiss will show him, will settle everything, as well as eliminate the tension that had been building ever since she'd opened the door and found him on the porch. It would convince Matt that what they'd had was over.

Finished.

Kaput.

It would show him that hurt and betrayal had taken their toll. That they had nothing left between them but painful memories.

"Libby. Oh, God, Libby."

It was all there in his smoky eyes, echoed in his voice... need, possession and a hunger so fierce she almost cried out. Before Libby could utter a sound, he jerked her against him and bent his head. The kiss was wild and hard and over before she was ready to stop.

Matt steadied her, cupping her face in his hands, muttering a soft, succinct oath as he took in her stunned expression. He gave her a quick, hard hug before he turned and walked out of the room.

Libby dropped into her chair, trying to take a steadying breath. She scowled at the empty doorway. I guess that showed him, she thought dryly. It sure did...that she'd wanted to kiss him. And what had she learned? That there was enough power in that kiss to light up downtown San Diego. And even more hunger. That Eli Trueblood and his crazy inventions weren't her only problem. Not by a long shot.

The telephone at her elbow buzzed and Libby fumbled with the receiver.

"Libby? How are things going? You okay?" Her cousin's vibrant energy flowed through the phone in quick, staccato questions.

"Hi, Carla." Libby slid down until her head rested on the chair back. "I'm fine. Just peachy keen."

"Uh-oh. What's the matter?"

"Everything," Libby said baldly. "The house is spooky, there are more severely dysfunctional robots walking the halls at night than I can count and Matt is here."

"Matt?" Carla went to the heart of the matter as Libby had known she would. "There?"

"Yeah. And no, he didn't dynamite the door. I opened it and let him in."

"Why? No, forget that. I know why. Because you're still crazy about him." Before Libby could argue the point, Carla was leaping ahead to the next question. "What does he want?"

"Me. Or so he says."

"Did you bother to remind him that he once *had* you?"

"I really didn't think it was necessary."

"Damn the man. He is the most stubborn, bullheaded, persistent and the most—"

"Unreasonable?" Libby offered with a wry smile, picturing Carla running her slim fingers through her short black hair as she searched for words. She sounded infuriated and probably was. She was also utterly loyal and as protective as a she-bear.

"Right. The most unreasonable man I've ever known. What he needs is a damn good lesson. Do you think you're as good a teacher as he is?"

"Me?"

"Yeah. You're not as ruthless, but you can give it a try."

Libby groaned, recalling a night six months earlier, a large bottle of wine, a sympathetic Carla and a number of painful admissions about lessons learned.

"Lessons," Carla repeated, savoring the word. "Like letting a man move into your house and your heart isn't enough if he's a traveling man? That love isn't necessarily a two-way street? That Matt's idea of a relationship isn't the same as yours? That the time he spent with you meant nothing to him? Does any of this sound familiar?"

Libby sighed and switched the phone to her other ear. "You used to like him," she reminded her cousin.

"Of course I did. The rat. That was before he packed his suitcase and headed down the yellow brick road."

Before he hurt you.

The unspoken words rang between them, an offer of comfort and unconditional support.

"Don't worry, Carla. This is only a temporary thing. Whatever the reason he's here..."

I came for you.

Libby blinked and tried to remember what she had been saying.

"Libby?"

"Yeah?"

"You okay?"

"Uh-huh. Just thinking. Matt's here because he doesn't like this house and seems to think I need protecting."

"Hmm." Carla's tone was grudging. "I hate to agree with him about anything, but maybe he's right. He's got a heck of a lot more experience with security than we do. Darn it, Libby, I told you we should pass on this one."

"Well, we didn't, and I'm here for a month."

"And so is Matt," Carla said dryly.

"Yeah, so he is. Right now, he's off dismantling a few robots."

"Robots?" Carla asked after a thoughtful pause. "Big ones?"

"As well as some teenyboppers."

"I *knew* I should've checked out that place with you." Exasperation vied with concern in Carla's voice. "It sounds like a nuthouse. When are you going to learn to say no?" They both knew the question covered more territory than Eli Trueblood's house.

"Next week," Libby promised, wrinkling her nose.

"Right," Carla said, her tone wry. "Does your weird inventor have anything else running around the place?"

"Would you settle for automatic flushing toilets? How about self-watering plants? Or an electric coffeemaker that always has fresh coffee?" Libby grinned, waiting.

Carla didn't disappoint her. "Always has fresh coffee?" she asked, awed. "And it's good?"

"I've never tasted better."

"I'm definitely coming over to check this place out. Oh, by the way, I got another call from your favorite yuppie at the advertising firm."

"Jason?" Libby groaned.

"Yes, indeed. Mr. Trent is still trying to pick your brain. The poor schmuck is way over his head in that job, and without you to save him, he's sinking fast. And there aren't any life preservers in sight."

"You didn't give him this number, did you?"

"No. I told him to take a flying leap." She paused and sighed. "Actually, I told him that you were very involved in your highly successful business and probably didn't remember enough of your old job to help him."

"Tactful, aren't you?"

"These days, it's my middle name. You never can tell when someone will need a house sitter. Hey, I gotta go. Watch your back, kiddo. Matt Flint is no lightweight, and if it's you he's after, you're looking at big trouble."

Four

Later that afternoon, Libby looked up from the magazine she was reading in Eli's living room just as Matt walked by the open door. Her heart dropped down to her stomach when she saw what he was carrying. The scruffy duffel bag was perched on his shoulder, balanced as easily as if it weighed no more than a sack of sugar.

Matt had once told her it was more convenient than a suitcase, that he took it everywhere he went. It had held his folded clothes and miscellaneous items when he'd moved into her apartment. And he'd stuffed them back into it when he'd left.

And now it looked as if Matt and his bag were taking off again.

"Matt!" she called out as she jumped to her feet and leaped toward the door. She wasn't disappointed, she assured herself. Nor was she dismayed. She was mad. Clear through. Even if he did look like a dashing renegade out of some old pirate film.

How many times did she have to learn this particular lesson? she wondered in growing fury. How long would it take before she understood once and for all that he wasn't going to be around when she needed him?

He had said he was staying. Damn it, he'd said he'd be here until Eli returned. And she had believed him.

Again.

"You called?" Matt beat her to the door and stepped into the room, his mustache tilting as he smiled. "What's up?"

Nothing at all, she thought, struggling with her temper. Just a small matter of betrayal and outright lying. Nothing to worry about. "Where are you going?" she finally managed to ask, keeping her fingers curled around the magazine so they wouldn't end up wrapped around his neck.

"Going?" Matt stalled, tilting his head thoughtfully as he gazed at her, not reacting to the question so much as Libby's tone of voice. Instead of the challenge he'd expected, she almost sounded panicked. "Down the hall." He nodded in the direction of her bedroom, narrowing his eyes and waiting for her reaction. When it came, it surprised him. Her eyes rounded but the alarm faded from them. Interesting, he thought, waiting for her next question. Damned interesting.

"Oh."

Enjoying her disconcerted expression, he prodded a bit. "Got a problem with that?"

"Exactly where down the hall?" she asked carefully, taking a steadying breath. "And why?"

He tackled her last question first. "Because now that I've eliminated Eli's wacky security system in this part of the house, I want to be able to hear you if you need help." He waited for a protest. When none came, he added, "And where? Right next to your room."

"Oh."

Her gaze didn't meet his, and when she looked around the room with a puzzled frown, he said again, "Is that a problem?"

Libby shook her head, frowning. "*That* isn't, and if it becomes one, we'll talk about it. But I think we definitely have one. A problem, I mean. Do you notice anything unusual about the walls?"

Matt lifted a shoulder to bounce the duffel bag into a more comfortable position. "Walls?" He glanced around. "They look fine to me. No cracks, no damp spots, nothing a homeowner could complain about."

"I meant the color."

He shrugged. "They're yellow. It's an okay color."

"That's the problem. They were green when I came in a few minutes ago."

"Are you sure?"

She gave him an impatient glance. "Yes. Green. I'm positive."

"They couldn't be. Walls don't just change color by themselves." He checked them again. Definitely yellow. "How could they—"

"You've been chased by a suit of armor waving a mace, and you can still ask? How do the plants water themselves? How does that coffeepot keep producing fresh coffee?" Libby paced the length of the room and returned to stand before Matt. "Eli Trueblood, that's how."

Setting the duffel bag on the floor, Matt nodded absently as he walked over to the wall. "You're right. And while the how is interesting, the real question is why. Why would anyone bother changing something like this?" He was still studying the plaster surface when a warm weight pressed against his leg.

"Hi, Sam." He rubbed the dog's silky head, smiling when Sam gave a sighing groan of contentment. His smile faded when the dog stiffened and moved away. He knew what he'd see even before he looked down. Sam was stiff legged, staring at the wall, his lips curling up in a silent snarl.

Libby moved closer, her heart thumping. "Oh, God. He's doing it again." Then in a strangled voice, she said, "And the walls are turning blue."

Matt cast a swift look at the walls, then returned his gaze to Sam, waiting until the dog gave a frustrated whine and eased back a step or two, looking puzzled. After swinging his duffel bag to his shoulder, he held out a hand to Libby. "Come on, let's get out of here."

"I don't like this, Matt. Not any part of it. Doesn't it make you nervous?" She clasped his hand and moved beside him, heading for the door, her eyes widening as the wall slowly turned pink. Sam moved with them, stopping to cast a suspicious glance at the far wall before he followed them into the hall.

"Nervous?" Matt shook his head and laced his fingers through hers. "Nope. Just damned curious. I'll go back and check it out once I get you and Sam settled in the office." He shouldered through the door next to her bedroom and tossed his bag on the bed, tightening his fingers to keep her from slipping away. "There's nothing dangerous in the living room that I can see. I'd stake my life on it."

Libby eyed him doubtfully and wished she had just a small share of his confidence. "Then why this?" She gestured toward his bag on the bed. "And why right next to me?"

"My move has nothing to do with the living room. Changing colors on a wall can't hurt anyone. And, if you'll remember, I was on my way before the show started in there.'' He dropped a hand on her shoulder and turned her in the direction of her office. ''I'm in the room next to you for the same reason I'm in the house. Because the place is an open invitation to burglars. Any kid with a credit card could break in here, and I sure as hell can't help you if I can't hear you. So you'll just have to trust me—at least on this.'' When they stopped outside her office, he looked at her. ''Can you do that much?''

Libby nodded slowly, looking up at him, taking in his taut expression. ''I'd trust you with my life,'' she said carefully. But not my heart. Never again my heart.

Matt's hand tightened almost painfully on her shoulder. It didn't take an Einstein to figure out what she wasn't saying. ''Then I guess that'll have to do. For now.''

Carla tapped her foot impatiently, listening to the bell grimly toll its message to the people inside. After long moments, the lock snicked and the knob turned.

As always, she charged in as soon as the door swung open. ''Well, I can see grim is the operative word around here. The gargoyles outside look like they're in excruciating and extended labor. And the doorbell. Good grief, it's enough to strike terror in the heart of a mass murderer. Does Eli have a vampire for a butler or—oh, it's you.''

Resigned to the inevitable, Matt watched Carla swing around and take a long look. Her expression wasn't flattering. Far from it. She wasn't thrilled to see him, and he couldn't really blame her. Not only were Carla and Libby related by blood, they were best friends. They had grown up living within blocks of each other, attended the same schools, mingled with the same circle of friends and were fiercely protective of each other.

Now she was confronting the man who had done the un-
forgivable, the man who had hurt Libby. She was no bigger
than a minute, but that wouldn't stop her. She was going to
give him hell.

"Yeah." Matt leaned back against the door and folded his
arms across his chest. "It's me."

"You're a nervy bastard, coming back here like this."
Carla closed in on him, going straight for the jugular. The
high heels of her red shoes clicked on the wooden floor with
every step.

Her short red skirt hit midthigh, making the most of her
shapely legs. Her white sweater managed to simultaneously
reveal and conceal. All in all, she was a beautiful woman.
Not in the same class as Libby, but beautiful. Matt knew she
was also a fire-breathing dragon.

"You do know that, don't you? That you have a hell of a
nerve?"

Matt nodded. She didn't know the half of it. And it had
taken every ounce he'd had to push his way in here.

After he'd walked out, it had taken him less than twenty-
four hours to figure out that he was the biggest fool in the
history of mankind. That there was no reason good enough,
no rationalization strong enough, no internal belief dark
enough to justify what he had done. He should have made
her put it into words, made her say to his face, "I want you
to leave. There's another man in my life."

Instead, he had wounded her beyond measure, and it had
taken him six months to find an excuse and the courage to
come back.

"I don't want you here," Carla continued, pacing back
and forth in front of him, glaring at him each time she re-
versed direction. "I don't want you anywhere near Libby.
On the other hand, I didn't know this place was so big—or
so spooky." She looked around with a shudder. "I hate to

think of her being alone in here, and to give the devil his due, I can't think of anyone who could protect her better than you."

Matt nodded again. Eli and his house had been the god-send he'd been looking for.

"But, so help me God—" Carla shook her fist beneath his nose "—if you hurt her this time, I'll...I'll hire a hit man to get rid of you once and for all."

Pushing away from the door, Matt stepped in front of her to stop her pacing. "I'll take care of her, Carla. You have my promise." And if he didn't, or if Libby kicked him out the door, Carla wouldn't need a hit man. He'd do the job himself.

"Carla?" Libby's voice preceded her as she turned the corner from her office. "I thought I heard your voice. It's about time. You've been promising to get over here for a week. If we don't get a secretary soon, neither of us will have a life outside the office."

Carla shrugged, coolly turning her back on Matt. "I know, I'm working on it, but things keep cropping up. We got a tremendous response to our last ad, and since you've been holed up in the mad scientist's castle—and therefore unavailable—for the past several days I've had back-to-back interviews with prospective sitters."

"How'd they go?"

"After eliminating the shifty-eyed candidates as well as the ones with possibly sticky fingers, not too bad. We've added twelve to the roster, and I've got more interviews scheduled during the week."

"Good work." Libby linked her arm through Carla's and tugged. "Come see my office. I've got the reports ready that I promised you. Did you have to dodge the peacocks on the way in?"

Carla shook her head. "Nope. All was quiet on the western front."

The two women made their way down the long hall, stopping so Carla could peer at the suit of armor. Libby laughed at her low-voiced comment, then said, "There's a lot more of them. Come on, I'll take you on the fifty-cent tour of the whole house."

"Good. I don't want to miss a thing, especially that coffeepot." She took a quick peek into the living room and shuddered. "I can't believe you've been in this monstrosity for eight whole days."

Matt could. He had shared each of them with her except one. One whole week he had been there. One quarter of his grace period. Seven days of heaven and hell.

Seven days during which Libby had done her level best to keep him at a distance. She hadn't succeeded, but she'd tried.

He had made his way through the house each day, examining locks, familiarizing himself with the creaks and groans of the wooden floors, studying the floor plans and wandering through Eli's workshop. Laboratory. Whatever he called it. The room was large, clean and so orderly it seemed highly unlikely that the man who cluttered the entire house with boxes and books actually worked there.

Seven days he'd spent trying to corner Libby and melt the icy shell she'd erected around herself. He'd made some progress there. Matt smiled grimly at the thought. If you could call making her nervous progress. It wasn't what he wanted but it was better than polite words and a cool smile.

The closest they had come to real warmth was the day he had checked out the walls that mysteriously changed colors. The answer hadn't been that hard to find—or that mysterious. He'd called her into the living room and shown her the lights cleverly embedded in the walls behind the ornately carved molding near the ceiling. It had obviously been done by the inventor, but Matt couldn't tell her how they worked or why.

Interest had drawn her closer and excitement had made her forget the past for a few precious minutes. She had put her hand on his shoulder and leaned against him for a better view of the lights. And he had answered her questions, saying whatever came into his mind, anything to prolong the time he had his arm around her and could feel her soft curves against him.

Hell, he didn't know what made the lights come on. And since they were all clear glass, he didn't know how they changed colors. But they did change. Every time he and Libby were in the room, they went crazy, flashing from one tint to another with dizzying frequency. As far as he was concerned, it was just one of Eli's wild ideas run amock.

And then there were the seven nights—six of them spent staring at the connecting door between their rooms. Listening to Libby move softly around the room, hearing the sound of her shower, the creak of her bed. Nights spent swearing because he knew her bedtime routine so well he could visualize her every movement. In his mind's eye, he could see her pat herself dry with a large towel before stroking on a lotion that smelled of raindrops and flowers. See her walk naked to the closet and take out one of the large shirts she preferred, then put her arms through the sleeves to let it slide down her body.

The dark of night wasn't his best time. It never had been—except for the nights he'd spent holding Libby in his arms. Now, if he wasn't listening to the soft, feminine sounds Libby made, he was hearing disinterested voices from the past, repeating the words that had first wounded then strengthened a young boy. Then later, words from his ex-wife that had broken an already cracked marriage. He couldn't escape the words any more than he could escape the fear that they were true.

Matt looked down the hall in the direction Libby had led her partner. In a world that was fair and just, words wouldn't have the power to scar a child, ruin a marriage or make a man walk away from the woman he loved more than life itself.

"Libby, who the hell are those men getting out of the truck?" Matt stood behind her in the doorway, looking over her shoulder toward the front drive.

She jumped. "Oh, you're back."

"I was gone an hour, plenty of time to drive to town and pick up some beer and stuff for sandwiches." He waited a few seconds then asked again, "Who are they?"

"Window cleaners. And, yes, they're coming here."

"I didn't think you arranged things like that."

Libby sighed. He had questioned her endlessly about her job. He knew damn well she didn't. "I didn't call them. Eli did."

Matt's assessing gaze shifted from the three men busily pulling equipment from the back of the truck to Libby. "When did he call?"

"I don't know. Sometime before he left."

"How do you know he—"

"Matt, I'm not an idiot. When the man came to the door and told me why he was here, I took his card, had him wait outside, and called the company. They verified that Eli had made the arrangements for this date. He even paid them in advance."

"Did Eli tell you they were coming?"

Libby rolled her eyes in exasperation. "Did Eli tell me robots walked the halls at night? Did he tell me peacocks screamed all day and ate fruit off the trees? Of course he didn't. He didn't tell me a damned thing before he left.''

"So you're going to let them in?"

"What else can I do? He wanted them and he paid for them. If I turn them away, they could probably refuse to come back, and considering the size of the house, he'd be out some big bucks. So, I'll let them in and keep an eye on them."

"Wrong." He held up a hand, trying to stop the argument before it began. "I'll watch them."

"You don't have to do that," Libby protested. "It'll probably take all day—even with three of them. Do you have any idea how many windows there are in this place?"

He nodded. "Probably better than you. But that's okay." He eyed the men as they strode briskly up the walk. "I don't like surprises, Libby. I especially don't like them in this house."

"Okay, if that's what you want," she said with a small shrug. "I'll be in the office if you need me."

He wanted to tell her to lock herself in, that the men didn't need to be distracted by her shorts and sleek top. But he restrained himself. Just barely. Turning, he walked out to meet the men climbing the porch stairs.

"Gentlemen." The men blinked at him in surprise. "You know that the owner isn't here." They all nodded. "My...lady and I are here to watch the house and we take our job seriously. So here are the rules for the day. The three of you work together in the same room and I tag along for company. Where one goes, we all go. Understood?"

"Whatever."

"You're the boss."

"The money's the same however we do it, but I'm supposed to do the outside windows," the youngest man, wearing a blue baseball cap, told him.

"No problem," Matt said calmly. "You do the outside. I'll stay with these two on the inside."

Libby, still standing by the screen door, listened with raised brows. Would she ever understand men? she wondered. Probably not. It seemed to her that Matt's explanation went beyond terse to rude and his *rules* were downright insulting, but instead of being affronted, the men just shrugged and set about filling their buckets with water from the hose.

There was something to be said for the blunt approach, though, she reflected as she headed back to the office. Many women would have worried about tender sensibilities or hurt feelings and never made their point. Others would have smothered the issue with apologies and felt guilty about observing the workers. All in all, it had been an educational experience.

The ringing telephone ended her contemplation and she picked up the receiver, saying automatically before realizing she wasn't in her office. "Sitting Pretty, Libby speaking. May I help you?"

"Libby," a smooth, deeply masculine voice responded, "you certainly can."

Libby held the receiver away at arm's length and stared at it, her eyes narrowing in speculation. When she finally put it back to her ear, the voice was far less controlled.

"Libby? Are you there? Hello? Libby? Damn it, Libby, answer me!"

"Jason? How did you get my number?"

"Well, it wasn't easy," he muttered. "I went over to see the Dragon Lady—"

"My cousin, Carla?" she asked sweetly.

"Uh, yeah."

"And did she give it to you?"

"Well . . . not exactly."

Libby dropped into her chair, resigned. Conversations with Jason Trent had a tendency to drag on, especially when he needed something and was prepared to cajole, beguile and charm all afternoon if he had to. If that didn't work, he was equally ready to whine and pout.

"So exactly how *did* you get it?"

"Well, as I said, I was visiting your charming cousin...."

Libby rolled her eyes and propped her feet up on the table. "And?"

"She was called out of the office and I just happened to see your name on a notepad with this number."

"What you mean is you went through her desk until you found it. Jason, have you no scruples?"

"Very few," he admitted with a sigh.

Libby echoed his sigh and leaned back in her chair, considering the man on the other end of the line. He had been hired by her manager at the advertising firm and had come to them with nothing beyond a beautiful résumé, a smooth line and lots of charm. She had been asked to train him, to "help make his transition a smooth one."

She had done an excellent job. So good, in fact, that he had used her expertise and slid into the promotion she had been expecting—and deserved. When she resigned, her boss had been astounded and expressed disappointment at her poor attitude. Jason had thanked her and moved into a larger office.

Now, he was up to his neck in hot water and yelling for help. A smile curved her lips. It couldn't happen to a nicer guy. On the other hand, he had been the catalyst—in the guise of the last straw—that had prompted her to make her move. In his own way, he had contributed to her present success.

So, she reflected, did she owe him?

No. She had given plenty at the office.

"Jason," she asked wearily, "what do you want?"

"Just a little information." His voice was bland again, as if he scented victory. "I'm working on this new campaign—the owner of the company, Mr. Wentzel, used to be one of your clients—and he doesn't seem to like anything I've presented so far. All I need is a little inside dope, the kind of thing he likes. Maybe some personal stuff."

Libby shook her head in disgust. Personal stuff. There wasn't anything wrong with Ed Wentzel that a good campaign wouldn't fix. He was a sharp man, knew quality when he saw it, even though he had his little quirks. Jason, on the other hand, wouldn't know a good campaign if it bit him on the nose. The only way she could help him would be to do it for him—and she wasn't that big a fool.

She listened to him pull out all the stops while she sifted through the various ways of turning him down. Finally, she settled for a leaf out of Matt's instruction manual.

"No, Jason." She settled back and waited for the next act. It didn't take long.

"No?" His tone was one of pure disbelief. "You're saying no? After all we've been to each other?"

"No," she repeated. "You got it the first time. Remember the word, Jason. It's a firm one. No negotiating. But just out of curiosity, exactly what was I to you? A mentor? A pawn? A fool?"

"Libby. You wound me."

"There was a time when I considered doing exactly that," she said cheerfully. "Castration was high on the list."

"Oh, Libby, Libby. What can I say?"

"Well, let's see. 'I'm sorry for double-crossing you' might be a good place to start."

"I never, *never* did that. They just knew a better man when they saw one."

The insufferable idiot. Libby shook her head and couldn't stop her soft chuckle. "No, Jason," she said quietly. "They just knew a man when they saw one. I wish you the best of luck, but there's no help here for you. You're on your own. Give Ed Wentzel my best."

She replaced the receiver, grinning. The boy wonder was in for a rough ride. Ed Wentzel didn't suffer fools gladly— or patiently. On the other hand, he did have a weakness— and if Jason discovered it, he might survive in the cutthroat world of Kendall's after all. Just as she reached over to turn on the computer, the phone rang again.

Picking it up, she said firmly, "Jason, I said no and I meant no."

"I beg your pardon?"

"Jason?"

"No. David Grant. I'm calling for my uncle, Jonas Radley."

"Who?" Libby's fingers tightened around the receiver. The voice was well modulated and male, but any comparison to Jason's ended at that point. This man spoke briskly, with a touch of self-assurance that promised to clear up the confusion.

"Jonas Radley, an old friend of Eli's."

"Mr. Grant, how did you get this number?"

"From Eli. He told us your firm was watching his house while he was gone. You're Libby Cassidy, right?"

"That's right, on both counts."

"My uncle and Eli have collaborated on several projects in the past, and they're working on another one now." He paused, then forged on. "Look, Miss Cassidy, this gets a little complicated. I didn't call Eli's number because he probably told you not to answer it, and he unplugs the answering machine when he leaves."

Libby nodded. That was exactly what Eli had said and done. "So you want to leave a message for him?" she said encouragingly.

"No, we want to come over. The day after tomorrow."

"Mr. Grant, I can't let anyone in the house while Eli is gone. That sort of thing just isn't done."

"I understand. That's exactly the way I'd want it if somebody were taking care of my house. But you don't know my uncle."

"You're right." Libby grinned at the frustration in his voice. "I don't."

"Imagine another Eli and you'll have a pretty good picture."

"Good grief," she murmured before she could stop herself.

His chuckle was a warm sound against her ear. "You're absolutely right. Uncle Jonas wants to drop off some papers for Eli—even though he knows Eli won't be back for several weeks. Don't ask me why."

Libby blinked. "That sounds harmless enough. I can take them and put them away for Eli."

"That's where it gets complicated. He'll hand you the papers. When you take them, he'll remember he has to change some figures. Then he'll ask you for a pencil. When you give him that, he'll need some paper, then a place to sit and a table to work on. Then," he finished gloomily, "he'll recalculate every equation on the paper, muttering to himself all the time. And it will take him at least two hours."

"Mr. Grant," Libby said, her voice quivering with mirth, "may I offer a compromise? I wouldn't hurt your uncle's feelings for the world. Besides, I have a hunch that Eli places a great deal of importance on this friendship. I can't invite you in, but I could join you outside. How about meeting on the side patio? We can visit there as long as we like. In fact, why don't you come for lunch? Around eleven-thirty? I'll have pencils and plenty of paper, too."

"Miss Cassidy, you're a lifesaver." His gratitude blended with wry humor. "Can I bring something?"

"As long as you don't expect anything fancier than a sandwich, nothing—aside from your uncle, of course. Oh, and make sure he remembers the papers."

Smiling, Libby replaced the receiver. Her smile faded when she thought of Matt's reaction to the invitation. He would not be a happy camper. More than likely he'd sit at the table, riding shotgun the entire time they were there.

That was his problem, she decided grimly. He had given her enough of them during the past ten days.

I came for you.

Four little words that had tossed her world upside down. Damn it, she had finally found some measure of peace. Healed the raw wound and started from scratch on a new life and career—neither of which included him. She had thankfully reached the point where she didn't think of Matt every single minute. Maybe every *other* minute, she admitted wryly, but that was an improvement.

What was he up to?

The first night in the house he had stated his intentions. *I came for you.* But he was the kind of man who went hell for leather after what he wanted, and he had done nothing so far. Except stir up memories and make her a nervous wreck.

There were too many memories, she reflected, moving restlessly around the office. Making love, his clever hands stroking her body, teasing, arousing. Holding her so tight she'd thought he'd crack her ribs. A rare look of vulnerability when he'd misunderstood something she'd said, the mustache-tilting smile when she'd explained. The unexpected flashes of humor, the quiet pleasure when she'd modeled a new outfit for him, the sensual intent when he'd taken it off her and carried her to bed.

She had been so happy. Her mistake was in thinking that he was, too.

Now he was back—and being remarkably patient. How much longer would his patience last? Not much, unless he had changed considerably in the past six months.

Of course, the big question was, what would she do when he finally made his move?

Five

Two mornings later, Libby shot up out of the tepid water with a startled cry. Visions of Eli's answer to the Loch Ness monster leaped to mind as she kicked for the side of the pool. As far as she knew, she was in the water alone, but she could still feel the tingling on her thigh where something had brushed against it. Something long and lean.

Matt surfaced before her in a geyser of foam and muscle, eyeing her with a teasing grin, then giving a gentle tug to the loose braid resting on her back. He tapped the center of her chest, just above the spot where the top of her yellow bikini dipped down, said, "You're it," and shot away.

Libby's eyes widened for an instant, then she dived after him, chasing him as she had done so often in her pool at home. The only difference, she remembered, was that she had always been the instigator. Right from the beginning, Matt had been too serious, too grimly intent on keeping his company at the top of everyone's list, to relax for long.

She'd had the feeling that his life had been long on work and very short on fun. Nothing since had changed her opinion.

Swimming was an equalizer for them. She was every bit as good in the water as he was. The only advantage he had was his height but she felt her agility more than compensated for several extra inches of reach.

The day she had taken matters into her own hands—soon after she had invited him to live with her, before he had walked out on her—had been a breakthrough of sorts. Matt had been swimming laps with his usual intensity when she cornered him at one end and wrapped her arms around his neck, allowing her body to drift against his until she had his complete attention.

When his gray eyes settled on her face, her heart skipped a beat. Matt always had that effect on her. He didn't just look—he admired, wanted, lusted and decided to have all in one quick glance.

"I have a suggestion," she had said breathlessly.

Matt's hands wrapped around her waist and pulled her snugly against him. "I'm ready."

"You certainly are." She grinned. "But I haven't told you what it is yet."

"Oh." His fingers slid over her bottom. "I thought you had."

She prodded him in the chest with a slim finger. "I'm talking about a game."

"Game." He looked at her expressionlessly.

She nodded. "Game. You know, things people do for diversion or entertainment?"

"I'm diverted right now, more than you know."

Libby's smile was brilliant. "Good. Now listen up. It's called tag. I touch you—" she laid her hand over his heart, admiring the sight of her fingers sliding through his crisp, dark hair "—and you're *it*." She had pushed away from him on the last word and headed for the other end of the pool, knowing he would be right behind her.

He was. And he played with the same intensity he did everything else, making her work to stay out of his way, then work harder to catch him again. She soon learned that having Matt following her was like having a patient shark tailing her, one that glided alongside her until the tension was palpable, then went in for the kill.

And now, following in his frothy wake, she felt the adrenaline pouring through her, increasing her speed. She'd missed the feeling, she realized abruptly. She had been so busy for the past six months pretending not to be hurt, she had forgotten one of Matt's major qualities—he challenged her, made her stretch, never let her settle for the easy path.

Pushing harder to compensate for his head start, she closed in behind him and stretched to tag his heel. "Gotcha," she muttered, and turned, kicking off at an angle and pulling herself down into the deeper water. It seemed no time at all before he was beside her, wrapping one arm around her waist and kicking to the surface.

They shot up, snatching air, breathing deeply, her breasts pressed against his chest. Matt bent his head and dropped a swift kiss on her parted lips. "You're it," he said softly and disappeared in a spray of water. She followed, remembering it had never done any good to complain about his unorthodox method of tagging. Matt made his own rules. They covered the pool in a blur of flashing arms, slowing to pull themselves down to the deepest point, then shooting to the top for air.

Finally, breathlessly, Libby called out, "Truce. No more." She settled into a lazy backstroke, admiring the blue morning sky through the glass ceiling, vaguely aware that Matt was swimming close by. Too late, she realized that they had fallen into a relaxed, synchronized, sensual pattern of touching, parting, stroking closer and touching again, choreographed by instinct and memory.

The dance ended as it always had, with Matt wrapping his arms around her, kissing her as they submerged and holding her until she forgot everything except the feel of him, and wrapped herself around him, returning his kiss. At the last possible second, Matt pulled them to the surface.

Libby clung to him, gasping for air, the past forgotten as she pressed against him, touched his hard body, gloried in his obvious arousal. Caught in the sensual tug of Matt's touch, Libby responded as she always had, heedlessly, drowning in emotion. His lips brushed hungrily over her eyes, her brows as she moved impatiently, trying to find his mouth with hers. When she did, they slipped beneath the water again.

Matt brought them back up and looked down into dazed green eyes. He dropped a hard kiss on her parted lips and took them to the shallow end. Libby rested her cheek on his pounding chest when he scooped her up and carried her to one of the wide lounges. His taut expression told what he wanted, and when he nudged the cushion to the floor she almost wept with excitement, sheer, shivering tension and relief.

"Libby." His voice shook as he lowered her to the cushion and followed her down. Her braid had come undone and her hair was a dark cloud of color around her face.

She shook her head and touched his lips with her fingers. "Don't talk. Kiss me. Touch me. *Hold* me."

Matt's arms tightened around her with desperate gentleness, touched beyond measure by her broken, murmured words. She wanted him. Libby *wanted* him. His slashing smile was exultant, savage.

It faded as quickly as it had come.

They would talk, he promised himself. Get the whole mess cleared up. Later. But right now he had run out of gallantry. He had promised himself when he'd walked through the front door that he wouldn't rush her, and he hadn't. And had spent almost two weeks' worth of days and nights in refined torture for his effort. Where Libby was concerned, even one day of waiting was one day too many.

She sighed and murmured when he removed her bikini top and tossed it aside. Her eyes were closed but he saw the pleasure on her face. His mustache brushed her satiny breast and she melted bonelessly in his hands. And when his lips closed around her pink, beaded nipple, he felt the jolt that shook her.

Matt slid the bottom of her suit down, his hand lingering over the curve of her hip, her thigh and calf. Tossing it aside, he turned to his own suit, salvaging a small foil packet before he kicked it off. His fingers tightened around it convulsively for a moment he was thankful for the habit he'd developed the day he'd met Libby. The passion between them had been so combustible that whatever he wore, wherever he was, he had protection for Libby.

Their kisses were urgent, hungry touches between soft murmurs. Seeking and finding. Challenging and comforting.

Demanding.

His tongue shaped her parted lips, moved between them. Tasted her sigh.

"Libby?" He didn't know what he wanted to ask, he just wanted the pleasure of saying her name.

"Umm?"

"Just...Libby," he whispered, covering her lips with his again.

He soothed her restlessly moving legs, stroking upward along her inner thigh. When he touched the warm honey at her core, he knew there would be no lingering, no prolonged teasing. Not this time. Not the way Libby was touching him. Hunger was in her fingertips as her hand drifted down, stroking, cupping until he thought he would explode.

He shifted on the cushion and she made a contented, purring sound deep in her throat when he eased down on her, resting most of his weight on his forearms. He laced his fingers through her damp hair. "Libby?"

"Mmm?"

"Open your eyes."

She shook her head, a slight smile curving her lips. "I just...want...to feel you," she whispered, rocking her hips against him.

"Honey," he said in a strained voice, "I really need you to open your eyes."

Her dark lashes fluttered, then slowly lifted. Her fingers tightened on his hips. "Why?"

"Because I want to see them when I—" he slid into her "—do this."

Her eyes widened, her gaze tangled with his and she gave a soft, helpless cry. "Oh, Matt."

Yes, that was what he wanted, needed beyond all reckoning. The dazed, love-drenched softness in her eyes, the burgeoning excitement. The soft cries. Her body clenching around his, demanding more. The blaze of passion. The hunger. For him. Only for him.

Libby slid her legs around his, tightening them around him as her body grew taut. She cried out again, convulsing, wrapping her arms around his neck and holding on as if she would never let go. Matt shuddered with a pleasure that neared pain, not moving, not wanting it to end, even as the ripples of her pleasure tugged, pulling him deeper within her body.

Finally, his body strained to the breaking point, he muffled his shout against the curve of her throat and felt the pumping rush of release.

Much later, Libby stirred, snuggling closer, lazily running her hand down Matt's back, stopping and flexing her fingers over the slight swell of his buttock, smiling against his chest when he shivered.

"Libby. Sweetheart."

There wasn't a soft spot on his body, she marveled. Wherever she touched, there was a powerful underlying network of sinew and muscle.

"Libby," he muttered, his lips touching her hair, her ear, her neck. "I've missed you so much. So damned much."

She moved her head restlessly, vaguely aware of the stream of words Matt murmured between kisses. She didn't want to talk, to listen, to think. She never did when she was this close to him. Besides, there would be time for that later. Much later, she hoped. Right now, she only wanted to feel his skin against hers, his heat igniting hers—again and again. Matt always made her feel that way. Fully alive. Feminine. A woman to match her man.

His arms tightened around her. "I'm sorry. I was a fool. I hurt you and I don't know the words to take the hurt away."

She nuzzled against his chest, smiling when she felt the rumble of his voice beneath her cheek. Well, now she knew what she'd do when he made his move, she reflected idly, trailing her hand down his thigh. She'd crumble—and do what she had been wanting to do since he'd walked in the door.

"Take me back, Libby. And I'll be the kind of man you need to make you happy. To keep you happy. Forever."

Restlessly, Libby moved her head. Intriguing as the vibrations beneath her cheek were, they were also a distraction. In the past, neither of them had spoken much when they'd made love—other than an occasional murmur of surprise or pleasure, she realized with fleeting surprise. Their pleasure had been in touching and being touched. It had been more than enough.

"Libby?"

She looked up at him, drifting back. "Umm?" Time to face the real world, she thought with a sigh. Too soon. Too blasted soon.

"Have you been listening to me?"

She smiled and shook her head, then rested it on his shoulder. "Nope."

"Why not?"

"Because then I have to think, and it hurts."

He flinched at her devastating honesty, then his arm tightened when she moved her leg from between his. "Don't go." His voice was strained with urgency.

"I won't." Not yet. In a soft rush, she said, "I haven't been with anyone since..."

Matt dropped an arm over his stinging eyes. God, how he loved her. Her strength. Her tenderness. Her courage. "I haven't, either."

"It didn't seem right somehow. I couldn't."

"I know. I never got close enough to anyone to even think about it." Matt put a finger beneath her chin and softly prodded until she was looking up at him again. He flinched. The hazy arousal he loved to see in her eyes was slowly being replaced by awareness and distress. His hand tightened on her shoulder in possession. He wouldn't lose her again. He couldn't. "Libby, do you think we could just take this one step at a time?" Her hesitation sent a blow to his heart.

"I don't know." She shrugged and made an encompassing gesture that took in their embrace. "How many steps do you suppose this was?"

"I'm not counting."

Libby half sat up, looking for her bathing suit, and groaned when she spied the bottom lying several yards away, the top even farther. There was no way in the world that she was going to walk buck naked across the decking to retrieve it. Not with Matt looking on. Not after a six-month separation.

"What's the matter?"

"My suit."

He looked where she was pointing. "Um. Yeah." The minuscule pieces of fabric looked like two splashes of sunlight on the gray tiled floor. "I suppose you have to have them."

She nodded. "Right now, it's a top priority."

Matt watched while her face turned pink. It still amazed him that she could blush, and at the damnedest things. There had been a time when she wouldn't have thought twice about walking over there to retrieve her suit. The flash of insecurity in her jade eyes was new. Another thing he could rack up to his treatment of her, he reflected bleakly.

"Let's try it this way." Before Libby knew what he was doing, he scooped her up and carried her over to the steaming hot tub and gently deposited her in the water. Then he turned away and picked up the bikini. *He* had no compunctions about walking around stark naked. He never had, she recalled all too vividly. He returned with the suit and a towel, putting them within reach, then bent down to drop a kiss on the tip of her nose. "I'll see you in a little while."

He turned and dived low and flat into the water. In less than a minute, he surged out of the pool, snagged his suit and walked through the far door. They would talk, he promised himself. It obviously wasn't going to be now, but it would be soon. He couldn't take much more of his gut being tied up in knots.

* * *

Matt didn't catch up with Libby until late that morning. She was peering into the refrigerator checking out the options for lunch. She had enough sandwich makings spread on the counter to feed them for a week.

"Oh, hi."

He watched with interest as pink tinted her face again. "Hi." He leaned against the bar and picked up an oddly shaped mechanical pencil and scrawled a series of dark loops on a scrap of paper while Libby pulled out lettuce, tomatoes and mayonnaise and added them to the things on the counter. "How many are we feeding?" he asked mildly, studying the point of the pencil. It had no lead. He drew a line through the loops and looked again. No lead, no barrel cap, no eraser, but it wrote. Obviously another of Eli's inventions. He wondered idly how many patents the old man had.

"Four. We're having company."

"The hell we are." Matt dropped the pencil back on the bar. "Do you normally invite people into a house you're watching?"

She shook her head. "Nope. I told you the rules of house-sitting. They're not coming in. We'll be on the patio. They're perfectly respectable," she added. "It's an old friend of Eli's and his nephew."

"Have you met them?"

"Well, uh, actually, no. The nephew, David Grant, called here the night before." She succinctly relayed the conversation to Matt, who had somehow metamorphosed into a cool, distant security consultant. "Then, I invited them over for lunch so the poor old man could deliver his papers. Is that a crime?"

"Maybe. Of gullibility. Libby, do you know anything about these two, other than what the charming David told you?"

"Well, no."

"Have you looked in Eli's address book to see if a Jonas Radley is listed?"

"I don't think Eli even has one," she muttered, fanning slices of bread on the counter. "He probably has a robot that spits names and telephone numbers out on demand. Besides—" she turned to him, waggling a sharp knife in his direction "—David knew my name, remember? He said Eli told him about me and Sitting Pretty. They're not coming in so why are you so upset?"

"I've told you. Because I think this is a house waiting for trouble, and since I don't know where it's coming from, I'm suspicious of everyone and everything." He tried the pencil again with the same result—dark letters, no lead. He definitely had to meet this eccentric old man. "What if they ask to come in?"

Libby sighed in exasperation. "I've already told David that they can't."

"And what if they have to use the bathroom? Are you going to point them to the shrubbery?"

"Oh. I never thought of that." She blinked thoughtfully at him. "Well, you can escort one inside and wait by the door while I baby-sit the other. There won't be any problems, you'll see."

And there weren't, he thought later. At least not the kind he had anticipated.

Their guests arrived promptly, following the gravel path to the side patio. Libby, wearing a green sundress and white sandals for the occasion, stepped forward to greet them. Sam, lying near the railing, watched.

"Mr. Radley, Mr. Grant." She tossed the ball in their court. "I do hope you understand about meeting out here."

"Call me Jonas, my dear," said the older man, taking her hand and bending over it, setting his shaggy white hair tumbling in all directions. "And David— You're being most kind as well as cautious. Eli would approve. David, come say hello."

His nephew stepped up and took her hand in his. "Miss Cassidy. Again, I thank you."

"Libby, please. It's my pleasure. I want you to meet my friend, Matt Flint." She slanted a look at Matt that said behave and got everyone seated around the glass table, David on one side of her, Matt on the other. Jonas settled a file bristling with papers in front of him.

Jonas and Eli had more in common than their white hair and an abstracted look that hinted they might be living on a plane unoccupied by mere mortals, Libby reflected. Their clothes looked as if they came out of the same grab bag. Jonas had on purple running shoes, one solid-green sock, one argyle, brown pants and a bright yellow shirt. Not one item seemed to fit his medium frame. He was in direct contrast to his nephew.

David was a bit younger than Matt, probably thirty-two or -three. His blond hair was brushed back and almost reached the collar of his dark, loose jacket. He probably had it trimmed every ten days to keep it that way, she thought, casting a glance at Matt's short, almost military cut. The only word for David was coordinated, she decided. Black pleated pants, slate gray shirt and a jacket that pulled together the two colors.

He was handsome, almost classically so, a complete contrast to Matt sitting silently in his conservative, sharply pressed gray slacks and light blue long-sleeved shirt, with the cuffs rolled up several times.

Libby smiled at Jonas. "Are those the papers you're leaving for Eli?"

"Yes." His hands tightened around the bundle.

"If you'd like, I'll take them in now and get them out of your way."

"A fine idea," he replied, hitching the bundle closer to him and riffling through the first few pages as if he'd never seen them before.

"There's no rush," she assured him with another smile. "Can I get drinks for anyone?"

"Anything, anything at all," Jonas muttered, frowning at a page he had pulled out and set on top of the pile. He withdrew a pair of glasses from his pants pocket, fogged them up and absently polished them with the paper he had been studying. "Miss, uh..."

"Libby," she said patiently, knowing what was coming.

"Er...yes, Libby. There seems to be something wrong with my calculation here. I wonder if I might borrow a pencil for a minute or two."

"Of course. Some paper, too?"

"Please." With a contented sigh, Jonas fanned the papers out around him. "Thank you, my dear," he said absently, accepting the pencil and paper.

Libby turned toward the door, quietly signaling Sam to stay. When she returned, Jonas was blissfully pawing through papers, muttering to himself.

"Real estate," David was saying. "Actually, I'm a developer. Custom homes. Just a few at a time for now. Later, I'll take on bigger projects. What line are you in?"

"I'm a consultant," Matt said blandly, accepting the beer from Libby with a nod of thanks. "A little of this and a little of that. A developer," he mused. "A risky business at first, isn't it?"

"Not if you don't rush things. Ah." David reached for his beer. "Thanks, Libby. Nice dog you have there." He extended his hand toward Sam and snapped his fingers. When Sam half rose and lifted his lips to reveal his gleaming canines, David snatched his hand back and wrapped it around the frosty bottle. "A little edgy, isn't he?" he asked, keeping a cautious eye on the dog.

"Just doing his job," Matt said before Libby could issue the scolding to Sam that was hovering on her lips. "He's a trained guard dog. Good dog, Sam."

Libby took a swallow of iced tea and slanted another glance at Matt over the rim of her glass. The message was the same as before—*behave*. She almost choked when Matt smiled at her and reached over to take her free hand in his.

"Yeah, Sam's a real tiger." His voice was as smooth as cream. "The perfect pet for a woman who goes gallivanting around sitting in other people's houses."

As if in confirmation of his comment, Sam rose and stalked over to the steps, looking down the gravel path. A growl rumbled deep within his chest.

Matt dropped Libby's hand, coldness replacing the lurking humor in his eyes. He motioned for Libby to stay where she was and went to stand beside Sam. "What the hell?" He turned to look at her. "More guests? Or are you starting a flower shop? If you are, he's carrying enough roses to get you off to a good start."

"What?" Libby rose and found herself securely attached to Matt's side. Sam's growl got louder as the visitor neared the patio. "Who on earth is—?"

The flowers lowered to reveal a good-looking man with black hair and bright blue eyes. "Libby, my love. I couldn't wait a minute longer. Tell your hound to cover his fangs so I can give these to you in person."

Libby sighed in utter exasperation and waved Sam back to his place by the railing. Gesturing to each of the men around her, she said, "Matt Flint, David Grant, Jonas Radley, meet Jason Trent."

Matt stiffened, David nodded amiably and Jonas completely ignored the interloper. Jason thrust the flowers at her and she went into the house to find containers for them, leaving him to fend for himself. He must be really desperate to soak this much into an investment, she decided, pulling large pickle jars out of Eli's pantry. There could be no other reason for the magnanimous gesture. The campaign must be in deep trouble—which was nothing new for him, at least according to the consensus of her friends still left in the department.

By the time she returned to the patio with still another bottle of beer, Jonas was at a table of his own with papers strewn all over the surface, and Jason was holding court at the other one.

"Libby and I go a long way back," he confided to Matt and David. "Worked side by side, in harness at the same time."

"You make us sound like a couple of draft horses," she said, smacking the beer on the table before him, wondering what else he had said. Matt's grim gaze shifted speculatively between her and Jason and back to her again.

"Ah, Libby." Jason took a mournful slug from the bottle. "Can't you see what you're doing to me?"

"No, but I can see what you've done to yourself." She looked around brightly and said, "Who wants a sandwich?"

Back in the kitchen, she looked at the prepared meal and wished she hadn't been so efficient. It would have been a terrific excuse to stay inside while Jonas was clicking right along on his calculator. And while Jason talked. Oh, God,

Jason. What was he telling them while she wasn't out there to defend herself?

Several minutes later, she swung through the open door with the heavy tray, asking brightly, "Who's hungry?"

David rose courteously. "Let me help you." He took a quick look at Sam, who had risen and moved to intercept him. "On the other hand," he said quickly, "maybe I'll be more help staying here, out of your way."

Jason bounced up. "It should be all right for me to help." He looked at Matt for confirmation. "Don't you think?"

"Sure." Matt shrugged. "If you don't mind losing a kneecap."

Two hours later—two long hours—Jason announced with regret that he had to leave.

Libby shot up, almost overturning her chair. "I'll walk you to the car," she said sweetly. Linking her arm through his, she urged him down the steps, turning to nail Sam with a narrow-eyed glare. "You stay there," she ordered between clenched teeth. When they got out of hearing distance, she lit into Jason. "All right, what the *hell* did you think you were doing back there?"

"Just trying to remind you how close we once were," he said virtuously. "Actually, trying to get you to help me with Ed Wentzel."

"Character assassination is not the way to go about it," she told him in disgust. The man was *dense*. "The way you made it sound, we were locked at the hips for the last six weeks before I left."

"We were. Practically. We spent all our time together."

"At work, Jason. During the day—from eight to five. And only because I was directly ordered to train you. Remember?"

He nodded. "And you did a damn good job, too." He noted her lack of response and changed tactics. "Please, Libby." His voice rose. "Just give me one more chance. Just a hint. You know the things that Wentzel likes."

Libby looked at his pleading expression and had an image of him hanging around her neck like an albatross for the rest of her life. Shuddering at the thought, she made a quick decision. Once more. Maybe it would get him over the hump and he'd either learn the job or leave.

"Okay."

"Okay? You mean it?" Before she could nod, he scooped her up and swung her around in an exultant circle. "You'll never regret it, Libby. Never."

Standing once more, she smoothed her dress and frowned at him. "I already do. Now listen. The key to Ed Wentzel's heart is animation. He loves anything that moves. The more things moving, the more he likes it. And jazzy tunes with clever lyrics. Remember the dancing doughnut holes he was so crazy about?" When Jason nodded doubtfully, she asked, "What's he pushing this time?"

"Low-salt pretzels."

"Okay, let me think." She stared down at her feet while Jason gazed at her as if she held the last key into the promised land. "How about this? A box of salt overturns and the grains form a chorus line. They start tap-dancing."

He pulled out a notepad. "To what tune?"

She rolled her eyes. "Make one up. They're dancing on a bunch of pretzels, spreading salt all over them. Then the bag with the new logo for low salt comes on screen and won't accept any of the pretzels, so the pretzels start dancing to kick off the salt. When they get enough off, they roll over and pop into the bag." She looked up. "How does that sound?" Besides insane, stupid and juvenile.

"Wonderful!" He leaned down and gave her a swift kiss. "You're incredible. I'll call you and let you hear the finished copy."

Up on the patio, Matt's gut tightened as he watched them. The man was an idiot, but he had Libby's full attention. What the hell was going on down there? This time, he promised himself grimly, he wasn't going to walk away from Libby. If Trent wanted her, he'd have to fight for her. Even then, it wouldn't do him any good unless Libby said point-blank that she wanted him.

"What do you suppose he really is to her?" David asked quietly.

"Someone from the past." Matt's voice was flat. "No one important."

"Good. Libby'd be wasting herself on someone like that." He eyed her thoughtfully. "She's really quite a beautiful woman, isn't she?"

"She's a lot more than that." Matt turned cold gray eyes on the other man. "And she's mine."

Six

"So that was Jason Trent."

"Yep. In person." Libby looked up from the computer and caught her breath. Matt was lounging in the doorway, his shoulder propped against the jamb. He had changed into his at-home uniform—jeans and a T-shirt—and it took every ounce of determination she had to keep from flinging herself at him.

It didn't seem to matter what he wore—a tux, business suit, jeans—his clothes looked as if they had been tailored for his lean, hard body, and he wore them with casual elegance. It was an elegance that men envied and women admired. Far too many women, as far as she was concerned.

No, flinging herself at him was not a good idea, she reminded herself. Especially not after what had happened at the pool. Probably not ever, or at least not until she had time to think about Matt and the future—if there was a future for them.

"I thought when you walked away from Kendall's, you would have left the advertising world and its people behind."

She shrugged and poked the save button. "Some of them still call me." With Jason leading the pack, of course, but his calls were the only ones she tried to avoid. "Some of them are still good friends."

"I get the feeling he doesn't think of himself as a friend."

She gazed at him thoughtfully. "You may be right. Frankly, I don't believe Jason knows *what* he thinks. Or feels."

"And how do you feel?" Matt prodded. "About him?"

"About Jason?" Her brows rose in surprise at the question. "I'll tell you, Matt. I have a very low threshold of patience where he's concerned. He was a pain in the butt when I was at Kendall's and he's *still* a pain in the butt. I don't usually bother thinking about him, and for the life of me, I don't know why we're wasting time talking about him now."

Matt's hooded gaze lingered on her expressive face. Her clear green eyes told him she was honestly perplexed. "I thought he meant something to you."

"He did," she said promptly. "Trouble. He was an assignment as far as I was concerned. My boss said to train him. I tried. He was hopeless. Good-looking, a great package, but hopeless." She smiled ruefully. "And then he got the promotion I deserved."

"And that's why you left?"

"That's right. I had been passed over for promotions before, too many of them. God knows you heard me complaining about it often enough. Jason was just the last straw. You must have heard me talking about him." She gathered a handful of papers and stacked them neatly in a pile. "But you know what? I feel sorry for him. He's in way over his head and sinking fast. He's in a flat-out panic over a campaign right now."

"Is that what this visit was about this afternoon? The flowers? The fast talking when he was leaving?"

"Uh-huh."

"And you offered to help." It wasn't a question.

She held out her hand defensively. "Don't start. If Carla learns about it, I'll never hear the end of it. I gave him an idea, that's all. Frankly, I think it stinks, but he's grateful. Now I don't feel guilty, and what he does with it is up to him."

"So he kissed you."

"Uh-huh."

"Out of gratitude."

She studied his face and gave a plaintive sigh. "What? You look like something's bothering you. You think I'm crazy?"

"No." If anyone was crazy, it wasn't Libby. And, yeah, he was *bothered,* all right. He was all but doubled up with pain.

Six months ago, he had walked away from the best thing that had ever happened to him because he had been waiting for the ax to fall and thought he saw it coming. Because he was crazy in love with Libby and feeling as vulnerable as a man could feel. Because his ex-wife chose that particular time to spew some poison at him and he listened to her. And because he thought Libby had found something special with Jason Trent—something she couldn't find with him.

Six months of unmitigated hell because he had been a blind and stupid—fool.

He ran his hands through his hair and shook his head. "No, Libby. You're a soft touch for a sad story, but you're not crazy." Hell, he couldn't fault her for helping that idiot, Jason. Especially since he was hoping that she'd be just as understanding with him.

"Matt?"

"Yeah?" He felt the familiar twinge in his stomach. He knew that tone of voice. Knew she was working up to something. Something he didn't want to hear. He could always tell when it was bad news, because she'd dance around the subject, tying his gut in knots before she finally got it out. It was a wonder he didn't have a full-blown ulcer by now, he thought morosely, watching her push back her chair and get up.

Oh, damn, she'd put on another set of those killer shorts and shirts. He wished she wouldn't pace, because he couldn't keep his eyes off the sway of her bottom and her soft breasts—and he had a strong hunch that she wanted him to listen, not look.

"Uh, about this morning."

He tensed, expecting the worst. Waited while she took another turn around the room, tossing uncertain glances in his direction.

"I don't want.... What I mean is, I can't..." Her words dwindled to a miserable stop and she slanted a frustrated glance at him. "For heaven's sake, can't you help me out here?"

Like hell he would. If she wanted him out, she was going to have to do the throwing. He wasn't going to volunteer. "Maybe I would if I knew what you were trying to say," he lied.

"Okay." She took a steadying breath. "Here's the deal. This thing this morning..." She waved a hand as if that would somehow clarify the issue.

"Making love?" he offered helpfully. "In the pool? On the floor?"

Libby closed her eyes, apparently gathering patience. When she opened them, her green eyes were filled with determination. "Yes. That's exactly what I'm talking about." She started pacing again. "It was too soon. I'm not ready for anything like that."

Yet.

She wasn't saying it, but the implication was there. Matt managed not to comment that she'd been more than ready at the time. Instead, he said, "What you're telling me is not to move my clothes into your room, right?"

Yet.

A look of unutterable relief crossed her face. "That's exactly what I'm saying. This morning was..."

"Inevitable?"

"A mistake," she said flatly. "It never should have happened."

"Damn it, Libby, are you saying you're *sorry?*" Matt swung away from the door and moved to stand in front of her. His voice was hard as he demanded an answer. "Are you? Because I'm not. Hell, I'm not a bit—"

"I'm not sorry," she blurted, turning away from him. "I'm scared."

"Scared." He considered the word as if he'd never heard it before. "Of me?" When she didn't reply, he said, "Damn it, Libby, you know I'd never—"

She spun around, cutting him off before he could finish. "What? Hurt me?" She blinked overbright eyes. "This may come as a surprise, Matt, but you already have." Almost mortally. "And I don't want it to happen again."

"Libby, I swear—"

She held up her hand, stopping him. "Don't make promises you can't keep. *I* would have once sworn that you'd never hurt me. I was wrong. You asked me the other day if I trusted you. I said then and I'll say it now—yes, with my life. But I . . . I don't trust you not to hurt me again."

As soon as she'd said it, Libby wanted to snatch the words back. They were true, she was scared . . . and afraid of being hurt, but she hadn't intended to open old wounds again—or to cause Matt's eyes to darken with anguish.

Matt flinched. She had finally said it, and it hurt every bit as much as he'd thought it would. What was worse, he didn't trust himself not to hurt her, either, and the thought was a pain deep in his soul. Tucked away somewhere inside him was always the fear that, one way or another, he would do just that.

He reached out and tenderly tucked a strand of hair behind her ear. Dropping his hand, he gave a sharp sigh and asked, "Libby, did you hear anything I said this morning? Anything at all?"

She shook her head. "I told you, I wasn't listening."

"You weren't listening," he said numbly. "It was one of the hardest things I've ever done and you weren't *listening?*"

Libby looked up at him indignantly. "Hey, I was busy at the time, okay?" An appalled look crossed her face and a flush began near her collarbone and swept upward. She touched her hands to her hot face and glared at him.

He felt as if he had just been put through a meat grinder, yet if she hadn't looked so genuinely distressed he would have laughed. Busy? Damned right she'd been busy. Busy climbing all over him, busy touching every square inch of his body and coming back for more, busy burning up in his arms.

Libby shook her head. "I don't know why, but you have this odd effect on me. I say the dumbest things when I'm around you. I'd be very relieved if we could change the subject."

IMPORTANT BEFORE MAILING...

1. Did you play your Zodiac Chart Game and Lucky Star Game? Did you print your name and address on the Game?

2. Did you play the Reach For The Moon Game for free books and a free gift?

PERF OUT AND PLACE HALF £20 VOUCHER HERE

Limit one 1st 50 award per household.

Good Luck!

THE READER SERVICE
FREEPOST
CROYDON
SURREY
CR9 3WZ

NO
STAMP
NEEDED

WHAT'S YOUR SIGN?

ZODIAC WHEEL

INSTRUCTIONS

Locate **your** Zodiac Sign above. Carefully detach and stick it in the space provided on your "ZODIAC CHART GAME". These Prize Draw Numbers could be **your** luckiest numbers ever!

GO FOR AN EXTRA £20 FAST CASH - NOW!

Can you find the other half of this £20 voucher? This offer is time sensitive - so be sure to respond <u>NOW</u> - you could be one of 50 drawn who will AUTOMATICALLY receive £20 IN GOOD OLD ENGLISH POUNDS! To play, detach this half of the £20 voucher, moisten it and stick it in the space provided beside the other half.

ARE YOU DESTINED TO WIN THE JACKPOT PRIZE OF
£600,000?!

CAREFULLY PRE-FOLD & TEAR ALONG DOTTED LINES, RETURN ENTIRE PIECE FOLDED IN THE REPLY ENVELOPE PROVIDED

ALTERNATE MEANS OF ENTERING THE PRIZE DRAW - NO PURCHASE NECESSARY

You can, of course, qualify for a chance at Big Money Prizes alone by playing all games except the Reach for the Moon Game or you may use these alternate means of entry: To enter the £600,000 Prize Draw and the Extra Bonus Prize Drawing, print your name, address and 'Zodiac' on a postcard and send it to: 'Zodiac', Reader Service, P.O. Box 236, Croydon, Surrey, CR9 3RU and we'll assign prize draw numbers to you. Limit one entry per envelope. To enter the 'Fast Cash Draw', print your name, address and 'Fast Cash Draw No. 3250' on a postcard and send it to: 'Fast Cash Draw No. 3250', Reader Service, P.O. Box 236, Croydon, Surrey, CR9 3RU. One entry per envelope. Entries must be sent First Class. This entry must be separate from any Prize Draw entry you are making. But why not get everything being offered! The Free books and Surprise Gift are ALL FREE - yours to keep & enjoy without obligation to buy anything, now or ever!

PLAY YOUR ZODIAC SIGN FOR A CHANCE TO WIN £600,000!

"In a minute. I may regret this, but let's get to the bottom line first. What were you leading up to?"

"That I'm in no condition to make any decision about us right now," Libby said with a sigh. "So don't crowd me. It's the only way we're going to get through the rest of the month. That is, of course, if you still intend to stay."

"I'm staying. I guess I'll have to keep saying it until you believe me. And I won't crowd you." Anyway, no more than he had to. He studied her face until she turned away and stared determinedly out the window.

The subject was apparently closed, he decided. At least as far as his favorite redhead was concerned. But things were looking up. He was still in the house and she hadn't slammed the door on the future. On the other hand, there was a world of hurt that still had to be taken care of.

Matt draped his arm around her shoulders. "Are you okay?" When she nodded, he held out his hand. "Good. Will you come with me for a minute? Actually, this is what I came in here for. I want to show you something. A surprise."

Willing to do anything that would break the somber mood, she unhesitatingly tucked her hand in his and followed him out the door. Hurrying down the hall with him, she thought of Sam's actions at lunch and tugged at his hand to slow him down. Matt obligingly stopped and looked down at her.

"What have you been doing with my dog? Trying to turn him into a Doberman? I've never seen him act the way he did with David and Jason. And you were no help with your 'trained guard dog' and 'losing a kneecap.'"

"I wasn't trying to be helpful. My intention was to protect you. I didn't know a thing about any of them, and if they had any ideas about the place, I wanted them to think a trained dog was on duty." He tightened his grip on her hand and started walking again, the subject closed as far as he was concerned.

"So what have you been doing with Sam?"

"Not much," he said vaguely. "If you remember, Sam has always been a matchmaker. When I'm around, he doesn't like other men near you. I've just been going over some of his original obedience work—sit, stay, you know the drill. He's gotten lazy lately, but I think he's enjoying the workouts." As well as learning a few new techniques, like guard and attack.

He stopped and looked in the living room before leading her in. "You sit in the corner over there. I don't want you in the center of things."

"What things?" But she obediently threaded her way along the serpentine path created by the chairs and plants to sit in the far corner. "You've moved all the furniture around," she said uneasily. "I wish you hadn't."

"Don't worry. I drew a plan of the room before I shifted things around. I'll return everything to its place before Eli gets back." He grinned at her. "Are you ready?"

"I suppose. You sure you wouldn't rather tell me about it?"

"If I did that, it wouldn't be a surprise, would it? Hold on a minute." Matt clapped his hands sharply and waited, watching the door expectantly.

"What are you doing?" For some reason, she found herself whispering.

"Hush. Not a sound. Not until I say so." He waited until she nodded, then turned back to the door just in time to watch the first little robot roll in. It was followed by another, and another, until eight of them were lined up before him. Not neatly or silently, but in a line of sorts. There was the metal equivalent of a grunt when the last one followed too quickly and collided with those that had already come to a stop.

They were the ones Libby called the whiz kids. Traveling silently—unless they bumped into something—they hovered just above the floor, automatically making slight adjustments as they moved from hardwood floors to rug-covered areas.

Eli had given them the type of eyes manufactured for dolls or stuffed animals and sold in craft stores—flat and white with a large, moving dark iris. Combined with softly molded noses and smiling mouths, they had an amiable, oddly lifelike appearance. Their bodies, rounded and sectional, looked like pewter snowmen, and their arms, surprisingly strong and flexible, resembled lengths of vacuum-cleaner hose ending with molded rubber hands like mittens.

Matt stood in front of them, waiting until they settled down. "Okay, guys," he said softly, handing them each a yellow-and-white daisy, "I want you to deliver these to the beautiful lady in the back corner. Go." Grinning like a proud father, he stepped back out of their way.

One by one, the robots swung sharply to the left and glided along the twisting path until they reached Libby. One by one, an arm extended, a mittened hand opened and a daisy dropped into her lap. One by one, they wound their way back through the room to Matt, lining up before him. The last one failed to stop in time and set off a chain reaction of bumping and clattering. Matt waited patiently.

When they were settled down, he said to the first one, "Turn on the lights. Go." The robot glided over to the wall, flipped the light switch and returned.

Vaguely aware that the walls were turning lavender, Libby watched as the robots performed their assigned duties—errands as varied as retrieving a book, closing the door, turning on a lamp and placing a magazine into a basket. Matt walked over to open the door and sent one robot to get Sam. It bustled out the door and a short time later Sam skidded into the room. He rushed to Matt's side and peered around him with a hunted expression as the robot following him slid back into place.

Matt patted Sam, saying to his squad, "Okay, that's it for now. Back to your places. Go." He looked at Libby with raised brows, grinning as the little machines slid out of the room. "What do you think?"

Libby collected her daisies and decided she'd be in big trouble if she told him. She thought he'd be a wonderful father. And she'd pictured him teaching a little red-haired boy with rain-colored eyes how to ride a bike, the hard planes of his face softened by love.

Opting for relative safety, she gave him an enthusiastic hug, a quick kiss on the cheek and moved back out of reach. "That's for the flowers, and the entertainment. They were wonderful! How did you do it?"

Matt shrugged and gave her a rueful smile. "I'm not sure."

"This is no time for false modesty," she informed him briskly. "They were better than wonderful. You could take those little guys on the road and sell tickets. Tell me about it while I get some water for the flowers."

Shoving his hands into his back pockets, Matt followed her out the door. "I really don't know how they work," he admitted. "Most of what I've discovered has been by accident. I was roughhousing with Sam last week and clapped my hands. Sam and the eight little guys all came at a run. I found out Eli had programmed them for vocal commands the same way. I threw a stick and told Sam to get it. He just sat and looked at me until I told him to go. When I said that, all of them took off." He grinned reminiscently. "Sam moved fast, especially with all eight of them on his tail. He got the stick, but he had a hell of a time getting it back to me.

"From what I've learned so far, the word 'go' has the same effect on them that the enter button does on a computer. It makes them move."

Matt opened the pantry door and watched while she scanned the shelves. Eli's idea of pantry supplies apparently didn't run to fancy vases. He also wondered what she'd do with the flowers. Jason's roses were still sitting on the counter in pickle jars.

"Eli is the genius behind the little guys," he reminded her. "I'm just trying to find out what they're capable of doing."

Libby pulled out a tall, thin jar and deftly arranged the flowers before adding the water. "So it's mainly trial and error?" she asked, picking up the jar and moving toward the door.

"Yeah." He followed her all the way to the office and watched with satisfaction as she placed the jar on the table next to her files. "Each day, I learn a little bit more about them, and each day they surprise me by their responses."

"Just think," she said absently, giving the flowers a little pat, "if you were in a different line of work, you could turn them into terrorists. Or bank robbers. Or—"

"Or since I prefer to stay on the right side of the law, maybe work with Eli's hatchet men out in the halls," Matt finished, giving her a thoughtful glance.

"Oh, Lord, I'm sorry I said anything." She turned in alarm to look at him. "Matt," she said nervously, "you're planning something. I know that look. Just remember, this is Eli's house and it's supposed to stay just as he left it."

He shook his head. "I think this job is getting to you. You worry too much these days. The look is hunger. What do you say to some Chinese takeout?"

Libby surveyed the empty white cartons on Eli's massive kitchen table with mild astonishment. "I can't believe we ate all of that."

"I ate more than my share." Matt picked up the cartons and took them to the sink. "I was hungry."

Watching him rinse and toss the cartons in the trash, Libby said idly, "You should have eaten more at lunch instead of sneaking half your sandwich to Sam."

"I should have, but after watching Jason and David drool over you, I lost my appetite."

Libby's eyes widened. "David didn't drool."

"In his own quiet way, he did."

"Hand me that cloth, would you? I'll clean the table." Libby chased down the last scattered grains of rice and herded them into her free hand, trying to ignore the sudden tension in the room. A conversation with Matt these days was a bit like walking through a mine field, she reflected. One second you were on safe ground and the next—ka-boom!

After dropping the last bits of food in the sink and rinsing her hands, she said lightly, "You sound jealous."

"I am. Jealous as hell. I always have been."

Libby stopped drying her hands and almost dropped the small towel. Staring at the stiff set of Matt's back, she unconsciously shook her head. Jealous? No, not Matt. Possessive? Yes, she'd grant him that—in spades. But he had too much self-confidence to worry about her being interested in other men. She watched him polish water marks off the faucet, lingering over a task that should have been finished by now and was just as glad that he was still turned away.

She took a quick breath and spoke before she lost her nerve. "Matt, you gave up any and all rights to me the day you walked out the door and left me on the other side."

"I know." He turned to face her and Libby winced again at the pain in his eyes. "Or at least part of me does. The other part won't even admit that the door is closed. It keeps telling me..."

"Telling you what?" she asked softly.

"That maybe it isn't too late. That I can find out what it is you need to be happy."

"And when you do?"

"I'll give it to you." His voice was flat with certainty. "Whatever it is, whatever it takes."

Libby stared at him, baffled. "Matt, my needs aren't that unusual. Things just aren't that complicated."

"They are to me."

Moving restlessly around the big room, Libby felt as if she were back in the verbal mine field again. What on earth were they talking about? Never in all the time they'd been together had they had a discussion like this. Matt, being a fairly typical representative of his sex, avoided meaningful conversations whenever he could, and having grown up with three brothers, she understood. He had rarely talked about his past. Only when confronted by pointed questions on her part had he mentioned his parents and his ex-wife—briefly, coolly and with finality. Seeing that they were painful areas, and reassured that his past had no bearing on their present, she'd let the subject drop and never reopened it.

Besides, she'd realized that men were often better at showing than telling. And in that arena, Matt had been exceptional. Never once had she felt unloved. As far as their relationship had been concerned, he'd been a man of few words, but the words had been just the right ones, spoken at just the right time. His silences hadn't disturbed her, probably because she understood quiet men.

It had been more than enough to see his normally cool gaze change to one of appreciation and desire when he was with her, to have his fingertips skim over her, lingering and stroking, as if she were a work of art instead of just a passably pretty woman. No, there had been no confusion about her needs or wants. He had instinctively known them—and promptly fulfilled them. With Matt, she had been happy and satisfied. She had thought he felt the same way.

But now, it seemed there was a definite communication gap and words were the only resource available. Before she consciously considered asking, the question popped out. "Why did you leave me?"

She waited. Silently. Uncomfortably. If she had thought about it first, she probably wouldn't have asked the question. But the hurt had never gone away. And it never would, she realized, until she had an answer. She had been too shattered to ask the day he'd left, but she wasn't feeling that way now. And apparently, even Matt was looking for answers.

"Why, Matt?"

"Because I was a fool."

Not a happy one if the torment in his eyes was any indication. "I'll take that as a given," she said finally. "But not as an answer. Were you unhappy? Was I crowding you? What on earth did I do?"

"You?" Matt looked at her as if she were out of her mind. "There was nothing wrong with you."

"Well," she said with gentle irony, "it's a relief to know that you walked out because I was so wonderful." Then in a wave of fury that shocked her, all gentleness disappeared. "Just what the hell do you mean there was nothing wrong with me? You packed, walked out with a so-long-it's-been-good-to-know-you, all because I was so terrific and had done nothing wrong? Please, I may be gullible, but I'm not stupid."

"All right," he said, goaded to respond. "God knows you deserve to know what an idiot I am. I went because I figured you'd be happier without me."

Libby blinked. "Without you?"

"That you'd be better off with someone else."

"Someone el— *Who?* Did you have a candidate by any chance?" Too furious to wait for an answer, she threw more questions at him. "Wait a minute. I'm missing something here. You decided this all by yourself? You got the idea, thought about it and made the decision without any discussion? You didn't bother asking me how I felt about the idea? I had no input at all? You . . . just . . . walked *out?*"

Matt ran his hand through his hair. "Look, Libby, I can see you're mad, and—"

"Ah. A man of perception. Yes, you're right. I'm damned mad. Because I didn't get to *vote.* That always makes me cranky."

"If you would just listen—"

"No." Tears glittered in her eyes. "You listen. For three solid months I wondered what I had done. I took full responsibility for whatever it was—the thing I'd done that was so terrible you wouldn't even talk about it. Then somewhere around the fourth month, I got mad. I figured that what we'd had wasn't all that good if you didn't care enough to stay and try to work it out."

"Oh hell, Libby. I'm sorry. I never wanted to hurt you." Matt started toward her and stopped when she turned the full force of her baffled rage on him.

"Didn't want to *hurt* me? You damn near killed me. But that was another thing I figured out. I'm a survivor. I can make it on my own. I'm not going to wallow in misery the rest of my life because of you or anyone else."

"Libby. . . honey." His voice was incredibly tender.

"Don't touch me, Matt." She held him off with an outstretched hand. "And don't interrupt. I'm telling you the story of a romantic fool. Of a woman who believed in Mr. Right and happily-ever-after. Well, you'll be happy to know that you've had a profound influence on my outlook. I don't believe in being vulnerable anymore. Or that love conquers all. And I will never, ever, put my heart on the line again. Not for any man."

Seven

Several hours later, Libby awoke with a gasp of terror, her hand shooting out to verify what her senses had already told her. A man was sitting on the edge of her bed, one hand on her shoulder, another firmly over her mouth.

"Mmmph!" Reacting instinctively, she lashed out with her feet and found herself helplessly entangled in the blanket, so she clawed at any skin she could reach and bit the hand on her mouth.

"Damn it, Libby, be still. I'm not going to hurt you."

An instant before the meaning of the urgent, hushed words penetrated, she stopped fighting. It was Matt. She would recognize his scent and touch and hard body anywhere. Providing she wasn't terrified out of her wits at the time. She slid her hand along his and tugged impatiently at the fingers covering her mouth.

"You okay?" he whispered. "You'll be quiet?"

She nodded irritably. When he removed his hand from her mouth, she grabbed it, holding it to her chest. "Don't you ever do anything like that again," she muttered between clenched teeth. "You scared the life out of me. I could have had a heart attack!"

"Yeah, I know." He patted her shoulder. "Sorry. But there's someone in the house."

"What?"

"Damn it, be quiet!" He started to slide his hand over her mouth again but stopped when her fingers tightened around his wrist.

"How do you know?" she whispered.

"I heard them."

"Them?"

Matt gave an exasperated sigh. "I don't know how many there are. Or exactly where they are—now. They're somewhere in the far end of the house."

Libby sat up, still clinging to his hand. "How could you hear anyone so far away? The walls are so thick you can't even hear what's going on in the next room."

"That's not the point right now, Libby. Let me go."

"It is too the point," she told him, tightening her grip. "How could you hear?"

"Because I bugged some of the rooms, damn it!"

Libby fell back on the pillow and studied his face in the pale shaft of moonlight that came through the window. It was hard and set, as grim as his voice. "You bugged Eli's house?" she hissed testily. "I don't believe this."

"Believe it," he muttered. "Now listen. I'm going hunting, and you're going to stay right here with Sam."

She shot back up again. "With Sam? Terrific. He did a wonderful job protecting me from you just now."

Matt swore. "There's no reason for him to protect you from me. He knows that, even if you don't."

Throwing back the covers, Libby swung her feet to the floor. "I'm not staying here while you go chasing burglars through the house."

"And where do you think you're going?" Matt found himself talking to her back as she rummaged in the closet, ducking when her T-shirt flew over his head.

"With you."

"With— The hell you are. I don't know what I'm going to find out there."

"That's just why I'm not staying," she retorted, wriggling into a pair of jeans and pulling a light sweatshirt over her head. "I'm not going to sit here like a nice little victim and wait for someone to charge through the door." She slid her feet into running shoes while she snapped the jeans.

"They won't get this far," he promised. "They'd have to get through me to get you, and believe me, they can't."

"There are some things in the world that don't know just how tough you are." Sarcasm laced her voice as she grabbed the heavy flashlight she kept beside the bed. "Have you ever heard of bullets?"

"Yeah, and that's exactly why I don't want you out there."

"You're not leaving me here, and that's final." She felt the wobble in her voice and grimaced, but she didn't stop until she reached the door. With her hand on the knob, she glared at him. "Well? We're wasting time."

Matt swore softly. "All right. You go, but so does Sam, and he sticks to you like glue. Tell him to heel. You stay behind me, and once we're out there—" he nodded toward the hallway "—you do exactly what I tell you to do. No arguing, understand?" He waited until she nodded and murmured to the dog, then he dropped a kiss on her lips and breathed, "Here we go."

Later, this will be funny, Libby promised herself as they silently crept down the dark halls, heading in the general direction of the pool. She shivered when she heard the ticking of the grandfather clock all the way from the entry room. It made the house sound so empty. And spooky. If this jaunt was scary now, she wondered, what would it have been like without Matt? She shook her head, not even wanting to think about it.

She kept one finger crooked in Matt's belt loop, even after her eyes had adjusted to the darkness, taking comfort in the heat and hardness of his body. His swift pace, as he led them through a network of hallways, surprised her until she remembered that he had decommissioned Eli's hall cops in their immediate area.

When they approached the pool, Matt stopped and turned until his mouth was at her ear. "When the robot on the right reaches the far end, we'll have ten seconds to get behind the hot tub, then when he comes down here, we'll go out the end door. The one on the left can't pick us up from where he is. Ready?"

She nodded. They reached the hot tub just as the robot made a military turn and started back.

Matt grinned down at her. "I'll have to show Eli how to overlap some of the patterns these guys make. He's left holes big enough for a semi to barrel through. Now listen, when we get through the door, I'm taking the long way to the other end of the house. I want to stick to the carpeted halls so the sound of Sam's nails on the floor doesn't send out an alarm. Ready? Let's go."

He's enjoying this, Libby thought with a shock as she trotted behind Matt. He was actually having fun. She tightened her finger in his belt loop and glared disgustedly at his back. Her heart was thumping loudly enough to rouse the peacocks outside and he was having the time of his life.

There was something radically wrong with a man who had reached the ripe age of thirty-five and still enjoyed playing cops and robbers, she decided. And as soon as she figured out what it was, she would tell him.

Matt led her through the house as silently as a shadow, avoiding the robots with an ease that would have depressed Eli. If he ever tired of the troubleshooting business, she reflected as he motioned her to stay on the carpet, he'd make a dandy cat burglar. Of course, having the blueprints of the house available and doing daily duty runs through the place gave him a distinct advantage.

Matt stopped and drew her beside him. She was aware of Sam's warm weight close at one side and Matt's at the other. Matt's large hand cradled the back of her head and urged her closer, his voice barely carrying to her ear.

"Eli must have run out of armor, because there aren't any robots in this hall, so we're the security system. I heard sounds in two different rooms at almost the same time, so I figure there's at least a couple people wandering around. I'm going to check out the solarium first, and I want you and Sam to wait in the small room off the hall just before we get there." He waited for her nod. When it came, he said, "Don't leave that room until I come for you. It's important, Libby. If someone comes up behind me, I have to know it isn't you. Understand?"

Libby nodded again, thinking he sounded alarmingly matter-of-fact about the possibility of someone creeping up on him.

"Okay. Let's go."

As they approached the solarium, they saw a dim light coming from the room. Matt shook his head in disgust, apparently at the carelessness of the burglar. Libby, with Sam at her side, went into the small room peacefully enough— until he began to close the door. She shook her head and made him understand that she'd raise holy hell if he didn't leave it open. When he turned away, he was aware that she'd edged into the doorway to watch him, Sam crowded in beside her.

As he glided the short distance to the small, glass-enclosed room, he pictured it as he had last seen it—sparsely furnished, at least compared to the rest of the jumbled house, with several plumply cushioned patio chairs and a well-used lounging chair, which he suspected Eli used for sunbathing. There were several tables with lamps, each crowded with stacks of books. Eli had put nothing worth stealing in the room. As far as that went, he reflected, there wasn't anything worth stealing in the whole house.

Matt paused at the entrance to the solarium, taking in the entire room in one sweeping glance. He stepped in, leaving the door open behind him. "It's always nice to see a man relax after a hard night's work," he said calmly.

A lean, graying man with a bushy beard, settled comfortably in one of the chairs, looked up from the book he was reading. "Evenin', young fella. Nice frog sticker you got there," he added, looking respectfully at the knife in Matt's hand. "But if you're thinkin' you need it for me, you're wrong. I'm a peaceful man at heart." A flicker of amusement lit his dark eyes as he carefully leaned the open book against his chest and rested his empty hands in clear sight. "Yessir, I surely do love a peaceful life. Benson's the name."

Matt nodded, feeling some of the tension ease from his body. "Flint. Enjoying the book?"

"Don't know." He looked down at the self-help book with another glimmer of amusement. "The man has some mighty peculiar ideas about fixin' simple problems. I don't know that sittin' around in a circle poundin' on a drum does much except make a lot of noise." He crossed his booted feet and settled deeper into the chair, his clean but worn jeans and dark T-shirt a sharp contrast to the flowered cushions. "In fact, I'm surprised the old fella even owns a book like this. Doesn't seem the type of thing that would interest him."

"What old fella is that?" Matt perched on the arm of a chair and waited.

"The inventor." Benson made a circular motion with his hand, taking in his surroundings. "The one who owns the house. Eli."

"Ah. Have you known him long?"

"Mmm—" Benson closed his eyes and thought "—five, six years. Met him in the park one day. Had a good, long chat. Spent most of the afternoon talkin' about this and that... you know how it is." He waited for Matt's nod of agreement. "He invited me here for a meal and we talked away most of the night. Ended up with him showing me where he kept an extra key to the room and telling me to drop in for a visit when I pass by this way on my travels."

"Extra key." Matt looked at him expressionlessly.

"Yep. Reckon he didn't tell you about it?"

"You're right. He didn't."

"Well, that's the way it goes when you get to be an old fella." Benson gave an expansive sigh. "You forget things. But that's neither here nor there. Back to my story. So I come to visit once, maybe twice a year—just for a night or two—and leave the light on down here. If Eli's in the mood for company, he comes down to visit. Sometimes he shows me what he's working on. Last time, it was some little robots, stood about knee-high to a gnat's tail and just sort of hovered over the floor. Cute little tykes."

"Are you alone?" Matt asked abruptly, thinking of the noise he'd heard in the other room. Benson might be exactly what he seemed—a footloose king of the road—or a distraction for something darker and more dangerous. More than likely the old man was all right, Matt reflected, but he wasn't taking any chances, not when Libby's safety hung in the balance.

"Alone?" The older man nodded. "Yep. Now."

Matt stiffened and studied the old man's expression. "Now?"

Benson nodded again, apparently satisfied with Matt's reaction. "When I came through the garden, real quiet like because I didn't want to wake those damned peacocks, someone else was out there. Youngish kind of fella, long hair, smokin' up a storm. I noticed him because of the smell—almost as bad as burnt rubber. Anyway, I rustled around some and he skedaddled. I hung around out there quite awhile before I came in—didn't want anyone to see me pull out Eli's key, you know—but he didn't come back."

"I think you'd better show me where Eli keeps the key." Matt put his knife on the table and stood up, waiting, curious to see how the old man would react.

Benson stayed where he was. "I'm thinkin' we've done a lot of talkin' about me and Eli and none at all about you," he said pointedly. "Maybe you'd like to tell me what you're doin' here? You see, I count Eli as a friend and I have precious few of them, so I wouldn't want anything to be happening to him." He gave a small shrug. "If you see what I mean."

Matt smiled. Benson might act and talk like a good old boy, but there was steel just beneath the surface. He'd be a good man to have at your back if trouble broke out, he thought idly, considering the wiry frame beneath the casual clothes. What he lacked in height, he probably made up for in speed.

"Eli went out of town for a month and hired my...fiancée's house-sitting service to take care of the place," he said abruptly. "She's baby-sitting the house, and I'm baby-sitting her."

Benson studied Matt with narrowed eyes, then got to his feet. "Well, I can understand that. I wouldn't let my woman—if I had one—loose in this place, either. Come on, the key's out in the garden. He's got this little statue with a hidden panel, and..."

Libby stood rooted to the floor, listening to Benson's voice dwindle away as he led Matt outside. *Fiancée?* The man was going to drive her crazy, she decided, running her fingers over Sam's silky head as she tried to calm down. And the worst thing was, he didn't even have to work at it. It was a natural talent.

Any man with a lick of sense would have realized after that scene in her office, that there was no relationship left.

None.

Zilch.

Diddly squat.

The trouble with that particular bit of logic, she reflected, was that Matt was an intelligent man. He knew exactly what had happened and what it meant. If he was ignoring the obvious, it was for a reason.

I came for you.

Libby's heart pounded at the thought and her reaction exasperated her even more. Surely Matt didn't think he could simply walk into her life—after walking *out* of her life—and just take up where they'd left off? Oh, he was trying to make amends, she'd give him that, but was his determination so strong and blind that he believed she'd put all the hurt aside and ask for more pain? Without any more explanation than he thought she'd be happier with someone else?

It sounded like it to her. Fiancée, indeed.

Well, she had news for him. It wasn't nearly enough. The next question on the list was *why* did he think she'd be happier with someone else. She was still fuming when the men walked back into the room, Benson's voice preceding them.

"Don't blame you a bit, Flint. If my woman was in the house, I'd pick up the extra key, too. Can't be too careful. If Eli wants me to visit again, he'll stick the key back out there. You want me to help you check out the rest of the house? Just to make sure that young fella didn't come back? I've gotten pretty good at dodging those big robots with the head crackers."

Libby tilted her head, listening to the deeper rumble of Matt's voice. She was trying to decipher the words when Sam stiffened against her. Quivering with tension, he looked to the left, away from the solarium, an almost soundless growl vibrating in his chest.

Sweat, cold and clammy, spotted Libby's forehead. This was not the time for him to start seeing ghosts. She crouched beside Sam and slipped her arm around his neck, immediately wishing she hadn't—she could feel his tension radiating through her entire body. She peered to the left, straining to see what Sam was sensing in his own way, through scent and sound.

"Quiet, Sam." Her whisper only carried as far as his ear. He twitched it and touched her arm with his cold nose as if in agreement. Libby took in a slow, steadying breath and almost choked as she spotted a shadow, black against dark gray walls, moving in her direction.

"I don't think so, Benson. Thanks anyway, but I'll check it out on my own. Get a good night's sleep. Oh, and don't go wandering through the house tonight, okay?"

Libby clapped her hand over her mouth when Matt's voice came so unexpectedly from the right. He was standing in the doorway, silhouetted against the light, his back to her.

"Right. Listen, with Eli gone there's no reason for me to hang around. I'll be leaving early in the morning, so I'll say so long now."

The figure—now definitely a man—was closing in with terrifying speed and silence. He slid past them without slowing down, heading for the lighted doorway, switching an object from his left hand to his right. Libby put her hand over Sam's muzzle when he shuddered with eagerness.

"Wait," she whispered.

She waited until the man paused several feet behind Matt, shifted his weight and slowly raised his right arm.

"Get him, Sam. Go!" The hissed command as she removed her hand from his collar was all the encouragement he needed. As she snapped on the flashlight, he snarled and leaped the few feet separating them, lunging at the man in an awesome blur of fury and coiled muscle.

"Matt! Watch out!"

"Behind you, Flint!"

Libby's scream blended with Benson's shout, Sam's menacing growls and masculine grunts. Matt and the intruder wrestled in the doorway, both trying to avoid Sam's snapping teeth. They fell into the room, scattering furniture like toothpicks.

By the time Libby reached the doorway, Matt and the intruder were gone. A wiry man with a gray-streaked beard was getting to his feet, holding a wicked-looking knife in one hand. Sam stood guard by the open door, looking out into the night, a growl rumbling deep in his chest.

"Where's Matt?" she asked, her stunned gaze darting around the room. Tables were overturned and broken, chairs tossed on their sides and a ceramic lamp shattered. Its shade had rolled to a stop against the outside door.

The older man looked up and nodded toward the door, but kept his voice soothing for Sam's benefit. "Outside. In all the confusion, your burglar got away. Flint told the dog to stay here, and I figured I'd do the same."

"Outside?" she repeated. "In the dark? You let him go out there alone?"

The man gave her a quick grin and sheathed the knife in his boot. "He didn't ask permission. Besides, I figure he can handle just about anything that comes his way."

Libby nodded, reluctantly agreeing. In spite of her concern, she had a strong hunch that if anyone was in trouble out there, it wasn't Matt. She took another quick look around the room. "The furniture," Libby said faintly. "It's...ruined. What am I going to tell Eli?"

"You can tell him the guy got away," Matt said disgustedly, walking through the door. He frowned at her, his gray eyes gleaming with anger. "You'd be better off thinking about what you're going to tell me. You promised to stay in the other room," he said evenly.

"Hell, Flint," Benson said genially, picking up a broken chair and setting it on three legs. "You wouldn't want her to miss the fun, would you? Howdy, ma'am. Benson's my name. You must be the fiancée."

Libby inclined her head, keeping a cautious eye on Matt. "I'm Libby. Libby Cassidy. And to answer your question, yes, he would want me to miss all the fun."

"Damned straight," Matt muttered.

She made her way through splinters of wood and ceramic chips to stand by the older man. "Was that Matt's knife you had?" was all she could think to say.

"No, ma'am." Benson shook his head. "It's mine, and a finer friend a man never had. That's his over there on the floor. When that young fella came flying through the door,

I pulled out old trusty Dan just in case Flint here needed any help. Didn't get to use it," he added regretfully. "I was afraid I might stick the dog instead. Mighty nice animal you have there."

"Thank you, Mr. Benson. I'm sorry you got involved in our problems," she said politely, gazing around the room in dismay.

His grin was a buccaneer's smile. "No need to mister me, Libby. Benson's just fine. And no need to apologize. Haven't had much call for old Dan's company in a long while. It's like old times."

Libby rolled her eyes. "This looks like a gathering of mercenaries," she grumbled, nudging Matt's knife with the toe of her shoe. "I suppose *he*—" she tilted her head toward the open door and the missing burglar "—was carrying something, too."

"Yep." Benson nodded matter-of-factly. "Came in with a cosh and wouldn't be a bit surprised if he had something more in his pockets."

"A what?" Libby looked at him blankly.

"Cosh." He waited for her nod of understanding. When none was forthcoming, he tried again. "A sap."

"Sap?"

He sighed patiently. "Blackjack."

"A rubber hose filled with lead," Matt said shortly, coming up behind her. He pulled a chair upright and shoved it behind her. "Sit." Libby did, and Sam settled beside her. "And I want your promise that if anything like this happens again, you'll stay out of the way."

Libby gazed at him through slitted eyes, tapping her fingers on the arm of the chair. "Of course," she said sweetly. "Even if another killer comes up behind you with a . . . a watchamacallit in his hand. I'll just watch and let you take care of him.''

"Good. Maybe you're trainable after all.'' He grinned when she gave an outraged gasp and leaned down to plant a possessive kiss on her parted lips. "Just kidding,'' he murmured. "About being trainable—not about staying out of trouble.''

Benson gave a crack of laughter. "Watching you two takes me back a few years. To some fine memories. And some rare fights. Ah, good times they were.'' He limped over to them and pulled up another chair. Settling into it with a sigh, he said apologetically, "A touch of arthritis.''

Libby nodded absently. "I heard you telling Matt you move around a lot. Are you a salesman?''

Benson grinned. "Just a traveling man. The last of a dying breed. A hobo. Traveling for the sheer joy of moving on to the next place.''

Matt pulled up the one table that was not broken. He sat on it and said, "We better get our stories straight before we call the police. Benson, I'll trust you to keep your knife out of sight.''

"Right. You gonna get rid of yours?''

Matt nodded. "For now. It'll simplify things.''

Libby looked from one man to the other. "What about that thing?'' She pointed to the blackjack lying on the floor.

Matt's gaze followed hers. "We'll leave it. It'll give them something to work with.'' He looked at Benson. "One last thing. Even though Eli's gone, you're his guest. We knew you were here. You like your privacy. That's why you're at the far end of the house. I think that covers everything.''

Benson nodded. "Sounds good. Oh,'' he added as Matt rose to his feet. "You better get rid of the bug in here before you call the cops.''

Matt grinned. Looking down at Libby, he asked, ''Can you think of any other loose ends?''

''Just one.'' She smiled warmly at Benson. ''If you ever want to settle down in a warm climate, I've got a great job for you.''

Eight

Two hours later, Libby stood by Matt's side at the front door, nodding politely when the police officer said goodnight. Benson sat near by, a benign smile on his face, a glass of Eli's brandy in his hand.

A second officer stopped in front of Libby, smiling down at her. "Okay, Ms. Cassidy, you're all set. We've had a few problems in this neighborhood lately. These big houses are pretty tempting." He handed her his card. "Feel free to call me if you have any questions. You're lucky your dog gave the alarm before any real damage was done."

"Thanks, Officer Kim, you made this a lot easier than I thought it would be. I'll be sure to have Mr. Trueblood call you if he finds anything missing." When she held out her hand to him, Matt shifted restlessly and Libby shot him a molten glance. "And you're right. I'm lucky to have Sam. Good night."

She closed the door and dropped into the chair next to Benson's, her eyes blazing green fire. "Well, you two certainly know how to keep the troops entertained, don't you? Sam heard the noise? You—" she glared at Matt "—were in bed with your fiancée and heard Sam? And you—" she turned to the grinning Benson "—turned on the light in the solarium hoping to scare off the intruder? When he rushed you instead, Matt appeared in the nick of time to chase him away? And why, for God's sake, did you take them around the outside and let the peacocks scare the socks off them? They almost shot them!"

Benson exchanged a masculine look with Matt before he reached out and patted her shoulder. "Libby, you have to keep things simple and logical when you talk to the police."

"*Logical?*"

He nodded. "Their kind of logic. You have a dog. The dog barks. Where else would your man be but in bed with you? And I'm Eli's friend—wouldn't I help? And as for taking them around the outside, they would've still been here at breakfast time if they'd gone through the house and run into Eli's hall monitors. So, it is logical—in a way."

"One of those man things, I suppose," she said in disgust. "Well, gentlemen, I'm going to bed. Alone. You two rugged individualists can sit up and do whatever macho kind of stuff you want to for the rest of the night. Maybe you'd like to carve up some more of Eli's furniture with your nonexistent knives."

Benson grinned again and shook his head. "I'm for bed. Flint, it wouldn't hurt to take a look at that knife wound. You just never know what kind of germs could be settlin' in. Night all."

Libby turned slowly and stared at Matt. He scowled back at her. His dark hair was rumpled, he needed a shave and he was irritable. She didn't care. "What...knife...wound?"

"Forget it."

She gave him a swift, assessing glance, her gaze stopping at his heavy cotton work shirt. It had been pulled out of his pants during the fight and torn.

"*What* knife wound?"

"I said forget it."

She stepped closer and ran a finger along the slit in the fabric. Her eyes widened. "It isn't torn, is it?"

"Libby—"

"It's sliced."

"Look, it's okay. When we fell against the table, he grabbed my knife and tried to use it on me. He didn't do a very good job."

Fear swept through her, chilling her to the bone, so she took refuge in anger. Pure hot fury. "That bastard sliced through your shirt, and you're telling me it's okay? Don't kid yourself. It's anything *but* okay. Let me see."

"This is stupid." In spite of himself, Matt was warmed by her anger, touched by the fear that caused it. "It's only a scratch. It didn't even bleed. Look at my shirt. No blood. See?"

"I said—" Libby spoke through clenched teeth "—let me *see*." She grabbed the shirt and ripped it open, ignoring the buttons that flew off and bounced across the floor. Her gaze skimmed over his broad chest and riveted on the thin pink line that arced from beneath his ribs to the center of his chest. The narrow line was dotted with dried blood.

Being careful not to touch the cut itself, Libby ran her finger parallel to the curving line. Matt shuddered and covered her hand with his, but she brushed it aside and traced the path again, her fingertips trailing through the crisp, dark hair, gently kneading his warm, resilient skin.

The next instant, she tipped her head back and looked at him with stormy eyes. "You could have been killed."

He captured her hand again to stop the tantalizing brush of her fingertips against him. "Well, I wasn't. You can see for yourself it's just a scratch."

"Scratch or not, it needs to be cleaned. Right now."

"All right. I'll clean it. Satisfied?"

Her scowl matched his. "No, I'm not. You probably won't do a thing about it, and God only knows where that knife of yours was last." She grabbed the hem of his shirt and gave a tug. "Come on. We're going to my room right now. That way, I'll *know* it's taken care of."

Matt followed her, his long stride adjusting to her shorter steps. Libby didn't fool herself...she couldn't have moved him if he'd refused to go. She knew he was indulging her, and she didn't care. She also didn't want to think. She was too mad and too scared to look beneath the anger to examine what else lurked there.

She marched into her bedroom and dropped Matt's hand. She turned on the lamp, pointed at the unmade bed and snapped, "Lie down."

"Libby, this is stupid. I've had worse scratches than this from taking a simple fall."

She whirled around and stopped him in his tracks with a look. "Maybe so, but you didn't get them because of me, so don't mess with me, Matt." She went into the bathroom and relieved some of her temper by letting the door of the medicine cabinet bang against the wall.

Eli's medical supplies were as ancient as his house. The dusty bottles with faded labels standing side by side on the glass shelves didn't look very promising, but Libby examined them carefully and finally settled on two of them. She hastily dampened a clean cloth and shook some antiseptic on it. Grabbing the other bottle, she hurried back into the bedroom.

Matt was stretched out with his hands behind his head, scowling, even with his eyes closed. He had shoved the sheet to the bottom of the bed and taken off his shirt but he didn't look happy. Tough, she decided, still riding high on the wave of anger. She didn't care what he was as long as he wasn't dead.

"All right, time to bite the bullet," she told him, sitting on the edge of the bed next to him. "Scoot over a little." Matt moved and she dabbed the antiseptic along the deep scratch.

"What is that stuff?" he grumbled. "It smells like old socks."

"Essence of newt's eyes and frog's feet. Be quiet and let me finish." She picked up the small brown bottle and shook it. "This might sting a little," she murmured as she trailed the small glass applicator over the antiseptic.

Matt sucked in his breath and swore. "A *little?* What the hell is it—lye?"

"Iodine," she muttered. "Hold still."

She was either going to kill him or cure him, Matt decided, tensing for the next fiery onslaught. Probably the former. Not with the iodine, searing as it was, but with her soft hands, trailing fingers and the fear in her green eyes. And he couldn't do a damned thing to comfort her, because she'd finally said it loud and clear—she didn't trust him. All she expected from him was pain.

Which was a hell of a blow for any man, coming from the one woman in the world he loved and wanted to protect. But she didn't want him to touch her. Okay, he could understand that. So he wouldn't touch her, but he wouldn't leave her, either. At least, that had been his intention after their conversation—until he'd heard someone prowling in the house and she'd insisted on staying with him. The combination of darkness, her closeness, the possibility of danger and her flowerlike scent had made him forget his hands-off policy—so he'd kissed her a couple of times and now she was mad as hell.

Actually, he admitted silently, he didn't know exactly why she was mad this time. She had several good reasons, and he damned sure wasn't going to open a can of worms by asking.

When a large drop of liquid plopped on his belly and rolled down his side, Matt opened his eyes. Enough was enough. Libby was taking her job too seriously, he decided, looking at the top of her head. Her coppery hair cascaded down, concealing her face and almost touching his chest. "Hey," he said gently, "you don't have to drown me in the stuff. I'm okay. You almost through?" Libby nodded just as he noticed that her hands were empty. He turned his head and saw the small capped bottle on the bedside table. Another drop fell and slid down his ribs. Then another. Matt reached up and parted her hair with his hands and groaned. Tears, silent and silvery, were sliding down her cheeks faster than she could brush them aside. "Oh, sweetheart," he murmured in a tender voice, "don't."

She sniffed inelegantly. "I'm not crying."

"Right."

"I wouldn't cry because you're stupid enough to get hurt."

Matt swallowed and cleared his throat, trying to remember if anyone in his sterile childhood had ever cried for him. For sure no one had shed a tear for him as an adult.

"Yeah," he encouraged, "you're too smart to do that."

"You're an idiot, and you're not worth my tears." Her voice quivered.

Matt cupped her cheeks and tried to stem the flow of tears with a brush of his thumbs. "You got that right," he muttered bitterly, watching the silvery trickles work their way over his wrists and down his arms.

"No, I don't," she wept, crumpling against him and wrapping her arms around his neck. "You *are* an idiot," she sobbed into the curve of his neck, "and I'm mad at you, but I don't want you hurt. Ever. I don't... know what I'd do if... anything happened to you."

Matt closed his eyes and held her until the shudders rippling through her body eased. His heart swelled with tenderness until he thought his chest would split. If this was all he ever got for coming back—just ten minutes with this redheaded tyrant clinging to him, telling him he was an idiot and dripping tears down his neck—then he was luckier than some men were in a lifetime.

And that's all he would ask, he vowed. He'd wait, and hope, and give her time, but he wouldn't push. He'd be patient and understanding, the kind of man she deserved. He would—

Libby's lips, sweetly touching the pulse in his neck, short-circuited his thoughts. His body moved convulsively and he gave her bottom a warning squeeze. "Uh, Libby?"

She murmured a protest and snuggled closer, settling on top of him.

She didn't trust him, he reminded himself. She needed comfort. She'd been scared. She needed to touch and feel to assure herself that he was still there. He could let her do that, he assured himself. He could control himself and just hold her long enough to let her lose her fear.

No, he couldn't.

She was going to kill him. If she had searched for a way to get even for all the wrongs he'd ever done, she couldn't have found a more effective one.

Libby traced his mustache with a fingertip and kissed his chin. He groaned and tightened his arms around her when her tongue touched the hollow of his collarbone. He took a deep breath when her hand rested on his belly, and slowly let it out when her fingers moved, lacing in the mat of hair on his chest. When her hand drifted back down toward his navel, he rolled over, taking her with him, and captured both of her hands in his, holding her motionless while he looked his fill.

Her eyelids were still pink, her lashes a damp crescent against her cheeks. When she lifted them, he sighed at the vulnerability in her overbright green eyes.

Libby blinked up at him. "What's the matter?" she asked huskily.

"I just want to make sure you know what you're doing, because things are getting pretty explosive here, and I don't want anything happening that we're both going to regret in the morning." He felt a shiver run through her. "But you have to know, the only way on earth I'd regret it is if you did."

Libby tugged against his restraining hands. When he released her, she placed a slim finger on his shoulder and pushed until he rolled back on the pillow, lying beside her. Staring up at the ceiling, Matt tried to convince himself that he'd done the right thing, the honorable thing. Hell, there wasn't any doubt about it—he just wished he felt better about it.

His heart almost stopped when Libby's finger traced the length of his zipper and she said, "I know what I'm doing." She rose to her knees beside him, sitting back on her heels. "I'm taking off my clothes, then yours, and we're going to love each other until we're too tired to move."

Her hands closed around the hem of her sweatshirt and she lifted her arms, slowly baring first her breasts then her face. She glanced down at him, turned pink at his look of unabashed hunger and tossed the shirt aside. Her deliberate movements were unconsciously sensual, not deliberately provocative. Matt realized it was simply her way of affirming what she had said. They had as long as they wanted. There was no hurry.

Even so, he didn't wait for her. While she wriggled out of her jeans, he rolled to his feet, kicked off his shoes, and with one swift movement disposed of his jeans, briefs and socks. He pulled several packets out of a pocket, then let the pants fall. He was waiting when she turned to face him.

Libby felt her eyes widen when she looked at him. Matt always took her breath away. Powerful and lean, tanned and dusted with dark hair that arrowed down his belly from his chest, spread at his groin, then continued down his thighs and legs, he was beautiful.

"I want you to remember one thing," she said breathlessly.

He nodded. "What?"

"I'm still furious."

"I know."

The words were hardly out of his mouth when she launched herself at him. He caught her and lowered her safely to the bed as he had done so many times before.

Each touch, each glide of fingertips was new, yet each evoked memories of passion and the irresistible need that brought them back together. Always.

Always together.

Libby flattened her hands on his chest and felt his heat pouring into her, warming all of the cold, empty spaces in her heart.

"Touch me, Libby." His voice was strained.

"I am." She dropped a kiss on his chest between her hands. "Where?"

"Everywhere."

Her lips moved in a small smile against his skin. "A wonderful idea," she murmured. "I will." She traced his mustache with a languid finger, smiling again when he pressed a kiss in her palm. Using the warmth he'd passed to her, she stroked, traced hard, sculpted muscles covered with smooth skin and crisp hair that still held a faint reminder of soap and . . . Matt.

She took her time, trailing her fingers across his chest, down the fine line of hair until it widened, until he tensed, waiting for her to hold him, cup him. Instead, she touched his thigh, his knee.

Everywhere, she had promised. And every now and then, when life was perfect and the planets were in proper alignment, a promise could be a wonderful thing. Libby rested her cheek on his pounding heart and smiled. Yes, indeed. A wonderful thing. With her mouth, she followed the trail her fingers had blazed, pressing her lips alongside the deep scratch, starting at his chest and working down to his side.

Matt groaned when her hair swirled over his aroused flesh, settling then gently teasing when she turned her head. "Enough," he gritted. "No more." Libby looked at him, her eyes rounded with uncertainty until he added, "It's my turn."

His large hands wrapped around her waist and brought her back beside him, with her head resting on his shoulder and her body pressed to his from shoulders to toes. He held her there, facing her, waiting until he could move without exploding. When he began to relax, she snuggled closer, draping an arm across his chest.

"Don't even think about going to sleep," he warned huskily.

Libby smiled, anticipation shooting through her. "I wouldn't dream of it."

His warm breath touched her cheek, then the brush of his mustache, and his lips settled on hers as if they had come home. Libby clutched his shoulder, clinging to him. He had always had this effect on her, turning her into a trembling mass of need with one kiss, one touch. And the reaction had always stunned her. Each time, she hoped and feared she would be immune.

It was still a shock—and unutterable joy—to learn there was no immunity. Not from Matt.

His lips touched her throat then discovered the tips of her full breasts, and she trembled, feeling lightning jolt through her nerves, sending shimmering waves of heat that settled low in her body. "Oh, Matt." Tension coiled through her, sensitizing her skin to his every touch.

Tears clogged in her throat, joyous ones this time, celebrating the gift of touch, his hard body against hers, the return of the one man who was linked to her for all time. Matt rolled on his back, taking Libby with him, steadying her until she sat on his belly, her knees on either side of his waist, gazing down at him. He grinned at her look of anticipation. "Do your worst," he murmured, running his hands down her thighs.

"Only my best." It was a promise sealed with the brush of her breasts against his chest and a kiss that took forever.

And Matt knew that it didn't matter how much time they had—a month, a year, a lifetime—he still had to have her right now.

Libby sat up with a dazed look. "Matt?"

His hands tightened around her waist. "Yeah?"

"Now." She rose to her knees and eased down, sheathing him with care, with incredible softness, whispering, "Now, *now*." Small internal tremors tightened her around him. She gasped, and Matt knew if he lived to be a hundred he would never see a more beautiful sight than Libby lost in her shattering response to him. Eyes closed, back arched, red hair a shimmering cloud of color, she chanted a litany of love, and with every word she called his name.

She drew him in, deeper and deeper, until he shuddered and his body joined her in the eternal dance, the meeting of body and soul. He surged into her, hands tightening on her thighs, holding her to him for all time.

Much later, Libby moved her head on his chest. Matt was still deep within her, his arm holding her close, and she sighed with utter contentment.

"Libby?"

"Shh." She dropped a kiss on his chest. "I'm not going anywhere. Go back to sleep." Matt reached out a long arm, turned off the light, tightened his arm around her and did just that.

Sometime close to dawn, Libby stirred sleepily. Matt's lips were at her breast, his tongue lightly stroking her nipple. She shifted, giving him better access, and smiled when he slid into her and held her close.

Later, drowsing in the curve of his body, his arm lying across her waist, she murmured, "I'm still mad at you."

Nine

The first thing Libby heard the next morning was the sound of someone moving around the room and a drawer being closed. She yawned and sat up, pulling the sheet over her breasts and holding it in place with her arms. Matt walked over to sit facing her, nudging her hip with his. In addition to being naked, he looked well-rested and very content. She blinked and held out her hand, lacing her fingers with his, and leaned forward until her head rested on his shoulder. "You're very energetic this morning," she observed sleepily.

Matt tilted her chin up and kissed the tip of her nose, smiling when she closed her eyes. He dropped light kisses on them as well. "I was putting my clothes away."

Libby's eyes snapped open and her hand went very still in his. "Oh? In here?"

He nodded. "I figured last night was the best invitation I'd had since last year when you invited me into your house," he said in a level voice. "The clothes are my R.S.V.P." Her blink of surprise made his voice tighten. He pulled her closer, tucking her head beneath his chin, only the sheet between them. "Look, I know part of you is still hurt and angry, and I don't blame you. I'd feel just the same. But another part of you—a big part—needs me almost as much as I need you. We proved that last night. I figure now is the time to do something about it. Don't you agree?"

Libby heard the edge in his voice and wasn't exactly sure what it meant. But, then, she wasn't sure of a lot these days. She nuzzled her cheek against his chest, stalling, thinking. She had lived with Matt for five whole months and was just beginning to realize exactly how self-contained he was, how little she really knew about him. During that time, he had managed—so skillfully that she hadn't even noticed—to answer her personal questions with the minimum of information and avoid talking about both the past and the future. She wondered if it was a natural talent or something he'd learned in the military. They had lived almost entirely in the present, and she had been so happy she hadn't even noticed.

He was so darned controlled, she reflected. He gave away so little of himself—except when they were making love. And then he gave everything. But could he possibly be as afraid and desperate as she was? Was he grasping at the same straws she was? Did he need time together to heal as badly as she did?

Libby took a shaky breath and exhaled against his chest. She sincerely hoped so; otherwise she was going to feel very foolish in the next few seconds.

Reaching for his other hand, she nodded, leaning back to watch his face. "Yeah, I do think we should do something about it, and I have a deal for you." She kept her voice light. "I suggest we use this old house as a sanctuary. We take the rest of the month for us. We have no past problems. We just live and—"

"Love?"

She nodded, tenderness flooding her when the strain in his eyes was replaced by a gleam of... what? Hope? Pure, undiluted joy?

Deciding she'd figure it out later, she rushed on. "Love," she agreed with another nod. "When Eli returns, it'll be time to face the real world. We'll go to my house and talk."

"It's a deal," Matt said huskily. He pulled her close, shaping her head with his hand and holding it against his shoulder, wondering if she would ever fathom the depths of her own courage. For a woman who no longer intended to be vulnerable, no longer believed in Mr. Right or happily-ever-after, who vowed she would never again put her heart on the line, she was taking one hell of a risk. And she was doing it with a smile—pretending that it wasn't such a big deal. But, whether she knew it or not, she was betting on the power of love with all her heart and soul. And he hoped to God she'd win, because if she didn't, neither would he.

"So," she asked, testing her teeth delicately on his shoulder, "where do we start?"

Matt released her and pushed the sheet aside, laughing when she let out a surprised yelp. He pulled her to her feet and hustled her into the bathroom. "With a long, hot shower."

It had been very long and very hot, she thought later with a private little smile as she walked between him and Sam on one of the meandering garden paths. She had forgotten what interesting things could be done in a shower.

Following a convoluted train of thought that took her from the shower to the bedroom to Eli's house to houses in general to house-sitting, she reminded herself to call Carla and see how the interviews were going. And they had to do something definite about a secretary. They were both getting bogged down in too much detail work.

Matt, she noted with an oblique glance, was deep in thought. He walked beside her, his fingers linked with hers, his steps matching her shorter ones, and he was a million miles away. It was a gift she had often envied, his ability to shut out the surrounding world when he mulled over a problem.

"Did anything about last night seem odd to you?" he asked abruptly.

Libby tilted her head and grinned up at Matt. "Ah, he lives, he breathes, he talks. Welcome back. That's a handy trick, disappearing like that when you think. You've missed all of my fascinating conversation in the past ten minutes." When he just gazed at her with narrowed eyes, waiting, still preoccupied with whatever thoughts he had been pursuing, she nodded. "Yeah, now that you mention it, a lot seemed odd. The fact that both you and Benson carry knives was really weird. That a break-in occurred the same night Benson appeared..."

Matt blinked thoughtfully. "Do you think Benson was working with the other guy?"

She shook her head. "Not for a minute. I think he's exactly what he says he is—a friend of Eli's. Don't you?" she asked anxiously.

"Yeah. I think he's okay."

Libby sighed in relief. "Good. As for the other odd things, I think it's extremely odd—and more than a little suspicious—that you are so good at lying to the police."

His mustache twitched when he smiled down at her. "I just try to keep things simple."

"Yeah. So you and Benson said." She gave him a worried glance. "Do you think last night was something more than a random attempt at burglary?"

"I don't know for sure." His fingers tightened around hers. "Logically, there's no reason to think so, but this little voice inside me keeps telling me that it is. I told you right from the start that I expected trouble of some kind."

"And do you always listen to that little voice?" she asked lightly, trying to mask her concern. It had been one thing to scoff at Matt's caution when she'd figured it was just an attempt on his part to get back into her life, but another entirely when someone had actually broken into the house.

"Yeah," he said laconically. "I listen to it. It kept me alive several times when I worked for the military."

Shocked, Libby tugged on his hand until he stopped beside her. "Kept you *alive?*" she repeated, frowning up at him. "I thought you were involved in security, with computers and things."

If she hadn't been prepared for it this time, she wouldn't have noticed the slight hesitation before he smoothly agreed. "I was. Most of the time." He gave a slight shrug. "But sometimes things happen."

"What kind of things?" she asked suspiciously.

Matt lifted one shoulder in another shrug. "Unexpected. Like last night. I didn't even get a good look at the guy." He glanced ahead and swore softly. "Let's cut across this way, quick." He nudged her toward the left. "That blasted peacock is coming, and if we don't toss him something to eat, he'll scream his head off."

Libby moved accommodatingly, wondering how often he had changed subjects just as adroitly in the past without her noticing. She looked down the path when Sam whuffed a greeting and trotted ahead. "Oh, look, there's Benson."

"Afternoon, you two." Benson looked out the open door of the solarium. "I was about to walk around the house and tell you I was still here. I overslept and decided to stay an extra day so I could clean up the mess we made here last night.''

''Oh, Lord, I forgot about it.'' Libby took an anxious look inside the door. ''Benson! You're a marvel. The room looks wonderful. You'd never know anything happened.''

He pointed to a pile of rubble beside the door, the remains of what had once been three tables and a lamp. ''I was about to get a wheelbarrow and cart that stuff out to the trash. Once I've done that, it'll look fine. Oh, I took some tables and a lamp from the other rooms to replace these.''

Libby stepped in and looked around. ''I'll come back with a notepad and you can tell me which rooms. I've got to make a report to Eli.'' She looked from one man to the other with a worried frown. ''Carla and I have never had anything like this happen, and I can't imagine what he's going to say. First we have gashes in the bedroom door from the robots, and now this.''

''Hell, Libby, the old fella will be so tickled his iron toys did their jobs, he won't mind about the door at all,'' Benson assured her. ''And he won't care about the tables. That's why he buys cheap stuff, so he won't have to worry about ruining things. That way, he can test his inventions wherever he wants to. He told me, as far as he's concerned, the whole house is his laboratory.''

''You've done everything you could do,'' Matt told her, looking around the room with approval. ''You called the police, made a report, got a case number. If he gives you a bad time, tell him he should have had better locks.''

''Uh-oh.'' Benson was looking out the door, shaking his head. ''We got trouble.''

Libby looked up from where she was kneeling to inspect one of the tables. ''Now what?''

"A pretty little gal is coming down the walk, dead set on a collision course with that damned peacock. He won't hurt her, but he'll sure scare the liver out of her."

"Good grief." Libby rose to her feet and started for the door. "I suppose it's someone collecting for a charity or something, although why she'd come all the way back here is beyond—"

An inhuman screech filled the air, causing them all to wince. It was followed by a scream that closely rivaled the first one—both in decibels and range.

"Carla?" Libby bolted for the door. "Omigod. *Carla*. Are you all right?"

"Libby?" Carla's shaken voice came from behind an enormous bush. "What the hell was that? A banshee? I swear to God, this place ought to be condemned. What do you do for an encore? Have Frankenstein's monster come lurching out the door?" She emerged from behind the bush just as Matt followed Libby out the door. Frowning at him, she said, "Well, I guess that's close enough." Her frown became a black scowl when Matt draped his arm around Libby's shoulders, and with the unthinking intimacy of all lovers, she leaned against him.

"Sorry," Libby said breathlessly, swallowing a chuckle. "It was that blasted peacock. We couldn't warn you in time."

"Can I talk to you for a minute?" Carla asked abruptly.

"Sure." Libby smiled up at Matt. "I'll see you later." She walked across a patch of grass and joined her cousin on the path. Linking arms with her and heading toward the front of the house, she asked, "What's up?"

"Several things. We have five new couples, so right now we're in good shape. I'm still interviewing, though. And I've written a rough draft of the ad for a secretary." She pulled a folded paper out of her tote bag and handed it to Libby. "What do you think about this?"

Libby scanned it quickly and returned it. "Perfect. When will we interview?"

"How about collecting résumés for several weeks and do it when you're through in the house of horrors?"

"Fine." When they reached the side patio, Libby squeezed her cousin's arm, giving her a rueful smile. "All right, go ahead, say it."

Carla sighed. "Damn it, I came by to see how you're doing, and instead, I saw *what* you're doing. You're sleeping with him, aren't you? Oh, hell." She gave Libby a swift hug. "Don't answer that! Forget I said it. I just don't want you to get hurt."

Libby returned the hug. "I know. All I can tell you is, I'm happier than I've been in a long time. And we're working on it. Right now, about the only thing I know is that Matt would never deliberately hurt me."

"And what about the last time?"

"Yeah, I know. He said he left because he thought I'd be happier with someone else," Libby said slowly.

Carla blinked. "He did? Hmm. I wouldn't have agreed with him then, but now I'm not so sure he wasn't right." Her smile didn't quite reach her eyes. "Well, Cousin, it looks as if you two have a lot to talk about. If that doesn't work, I have a shoulder to cry on if you need it."

"I know. I've always known." They stood by Carla's white Buick, each bringing the other up to date on their individual projects. "Oh," Libby ended, "you'll be delighted with this bit of news. We had a break-in last night and some furniture was broken."

"Oh, my God. Are we liable?"

"No." Libby grinned. "If necessary, Matt, in his official capacity, will swear that the locks are inadequate, so we're off the hook." She sobered and said, "But there's one thing more."

Carla groaned. "What?"

"I need to know how you're going to act if Matt and I fix things up. Are we going to have to stand outside and talk to each other because you can't bear to be around him?" Libby blinked and stared at the car. "Don't make me choose between you and him. Please."

"Oh, Libby, I'd never do that!" Carla gave her cousin another fierce hug. "I promise, the minute I know he's staying and you're happy, I'll give him a kiss he'll never forget and welcome him back to the fold. Satisfied?"

Libby nodded and waited until Carla slid behind the wheel and closed the door. "Carla?"

"Hmm?"

"A hug will do just fine."

Carla laughed, waggled her fingers in a farewell wave and took off with her usual flair. Libby trotted up the porch stairs and found Matt waiting by the door. He opened the screen and studied her face.

"Are you okay?"

She smiled, hoping to alleviate the concern in his eyes. "I'm wonderful. Did I hear the phone ringing while I was out there?"

Matt nodded. "Two messages for you. Your yuppie friend called and said Ed liked the idea and they'll be discussing it over lunch. Ed's paying. Is there a special significance to that?"

Libby grinned. "It means that Jason isn't in quite so far over his head anymore. And the second?"

"David called."

"And?"

"He wanted to take you out to lunch, to thank you for your graciousness with his uncle. I told him that I'd convey his thanks, but you wouldn't be interested in the lunch. I also told him not to bother calling back, that my woman doesn't go out—for meals or anything else—with other men."

Libby's brows arched, but she couldn't keep from grinning. "Acting a tad possessive, aren't you, Mr. Flint?"

"Indeed I am, Ms. Cassidy. I always have been. I'm surprised you never noticed." When she laughed, he held out his hand, saying, "Come to the living room with me. I want you to try something."

"I see you have the troops assembled," she commented as they entered the room. In the area Matt had cleared for them, the whiz kids were lined up as if awaiting inspection. Sam stared at the green wall with rapt concentration.

"Yeah, I've been working with them. Watch this." Matt gave a number of low-voiced commands in rapid order, ending with the order to "go." Silently, the robots rolled away, each performing a different operation. When they finished, they returned to line up in front of Matt. He looked at Libby. "Well, what do you think?"

"I think they're more sophisticated than they were the last time you did this. Yesterday, you gave each one an individual order. Today you give general instructions and somehow they sort them out between them, each one doing a different task." She turned to him with a puzzled frown. "Is that possible?"

"Apparently." He shrugged. "But don't ask me how. Maybe I'm making my commands clearer. Now I want you to try the same thing."

She looked up in automatic protest. "But, I haven't been working with them."

"Exactly. That's why I want to see if they'll take orders from you. Here's the list of things I told them to do. Go on, read it."

"But—"

"Come on, Libby, just do it!"

With a long-suffering sigh, she obediently read the list, adding a firm "go." Her eyes rounded in astonishment when they moved, repeating the tasks they had performed earlier. "Good grief," she whispered. "They did it."

"Yeah." Matt eyed the ragtag line thoughtfully. "Now the question is, will they do it for anyone else? I'm going to get Benson. Be back in a minute."

While he was gone, Libby entertained herself by reading the list again and watching the little robots scurry about their designated tasks. They were just forming a line before her when the two men arrived.

"Hey, look at that!" Benson watched in delight as they skittered into place. "He's really got them working! Okay, what do you want me to do?" Libby handed him the list and Benson read it, adding the final command when prompted by Matt. His disappointment was palpable when the robots remained motionless. "Heck. I wanted to see if old Eli had pulled off even half the things he had planned for them."

Matt looked thoughtful. "That's two out of three," he murmured. "I wish we had someone else around here to test."

A deep gong reverberated down the hallway and Libby looked at Matt. "I'll get it. Why don't you let the little guys show off for Benson?" As she walked down the hall, Matt was giving the robots their next set of orders. Libby pulled open the door and looked out. "Jason! What are you doing here?"

He handed her another lavish spray of roses and stepped into the hallway. "I just had lunch with Ed Wentzel. He loves the idea. I just wanted you to know, and to say thank you."

"You're very welcome." She took the flowers, wondering if Eli had any more pickle jars.

"And to tell you that I owe you," he finished. "If there's ever anything I can do for you, just—"

"Libby, who is it?" Matt stepped into the hallway. "Oh, you." His tone would have discouraged a less self-absorbed man.

"Matt," Libby said brightly, "Jason just dropped by to say thank you. Isn't that nice?"

"Peachy."

"Maybe while he's here, he'll help us with the little test we're running in the living room."

Jason reached for the doorknob. "I've, uh, never been very good at tests. Maybe you should get someone else."

Libby slipped her arm through his and urged him down the hall toward Matt. "It's not really a test," she said soothingly. "It's really more of a . . . a demonstration. Isn't that right, Matt?"

"Right," he said dryly. "Why don't you explain it to him while I check things out in here." His narrow-eyed glance warned her that her explanation had better be good— meaning that it should contain no reference to robots or anything that affected the security of the house.

Libby gave Jason a bright smile that covered her racing thoughts. "It's really very simple. The owner of this place is an eccentric inventor who . . . has a number of very interesting inventions in the house," she said lamely. "We found a list that sounds like instructions and, uh, we're trying to see if any of the stuff is voice activated."

Jason frowned. "Why—"

"Oh, I know it's none of our business," Libby said hurriedly. "We're just curious. Maybe nosy is a better word. Anyway, we tried reading it and nothing happened, so we just thought it would be nice if someone else could try. And here you are!'' She hustled him into the room, ignoring both Matt's sardonic expression and Benson's amusement. ''Jason, this is Mr. Benson, a friend,'' she said briefly, stopping just inside the door.

He nodded politely but his gaze was on the eight robots. ''What are those?''

Libby's frazzled glance moved from Matt to Benson imploringly. They shrugged, as if to remind her it was her show.

''Uh . . . sculptures!'' she said brightly. ''The owner is a collector. Matt, where's that list? I'm sure Jason is in a hurry. He's got a lot to do.''

''Libby?'' Jason's gaze was puzzled. ''Do you know your dog is growling at the wall?''

She rolled her eyes and snatched the paper from Matt. ''Yes, he does it a lot. I think there might be mice in the walls. Here.'' She turned Jason until his back was to the robots. ''Read this.''

And God help her if the robots moved before she could get Jason out of the room, she thought after a quick peek at Matt's frown. Benson, as always, was amused.

She held her breath while Jason read, letting it out in a rush when nothing happened. ''Well, I guess we were wrong. Nothing's different.''

''Except that the walls are changing color,'' Jason observed as he slowly turned and checked them all.

Libby took the paper from him and slipped it into her pocket. ''They do that all the time,'' she said absently, linking her arm through his and leading him back to the front door. ''Thanks for giving us a hand. You were a big help.''

''I still don't understand—''

''Neither do we,'' she interrupted ruthlessly, opening the door. ''Good luck on the campaign, and give Ed Wentzel my best the next time you have lunch with him." She closed the door and hurried back to the living room. "You two were sure a lot of help," she grumbled as she entered the room. "Oh, where's Benson?"

"The excitement was too much for him," Matt said dryly. "He went back to his book. Sam decided to take a nap over there under the table."

"So, what do you think?" she asked, perching on the arm of his chair.

He reached up to ruffle her hair. "I think you have a real way with words and Jason's as dumb as dirt if he believed a word of it."

"Not that." She batted his hand away and slid down into his lap. "About the whiz kids."

"I think they're programmed to our voices—yours and mine—and although I understand a bit about electronics, I can't understand how it was done. They also seem to be getting smarter every day, but that's impossible."

Libby dropped her head on his shoulder, relishing his quiet strength, cherishing the fact that she could once again touch and be held by him. She looked at the ceiling, saying thoughtfully, "I'm getting a long list of questions that I want to ask Eli when he gets back."

"Me, too." Matt made a contented sound and ran his large hand down her bare leg. "Have I told you I'm crazy about these shorts?"

"Good. I aim to please."

"You do. Very much."

Libby touched his mustache, stroking it with her finger, lost in the wonder of being so close. Her hand brushed his cheek and without warning tears burned her eyes. She could hold her own with Matt when he was being possessive or just plain maddening, she told herself, swallowing to relieve the tension in her throat, but it was these quiet moments when she was most vulnerable—when he was simply holding her and she realized just how much they had lost.

Matt stiffened, brushing her cheek with his thumb. "What's the matter?"

"Nothing." She shook her head, blinking. "I'm just being silly."

"Tell me, sweetheart. Trust me enough to tell me."

"I've just…missed you so…much." And that fast, need tore through her. Need and remembered emptiness and a sudden, terrible fear. She turned and feverishly wrapped her arms around Matt's neck. "Hold me. Tight. Don't ever let me go."

His lips met hers in a kiss that was meant to be soothing, reassuring, but its fire and urgency jolted right down to her toes. Tears dried in its heat and Libby's pulse thrummed exultantly. Tenderness, hunger, determination, regret—she tasted them all in his searing kisses, as well as a promise of joy and hope.

And behind them, the wall turned an ever-deepening red, eventually settling into a constant crimson flicker. A soft popping sound attracted Sam's attention and he left the underside of the table to investigate. He nosed a small bulb near the baseboard, then stiffened and stared at the wall, growling.

Matt tightened his arms protectively around Libby, murmuring, "Sam sounds like he's going to tear the place down." Lifting his head, he stared in disbelief at the flashing crimson wall, then nudged Libby. "You've got to see this. Eli has outdone himself."

Later that evening, when Matt walked to the living room to wait for Libby, he stopped in the doorway, taking in the scene before him. The walls were once again green. A slight, gray-haired man stood high on a ladder, briskly replacing bulbs almost hidden in the recesses of the carved molding near the ceiling.

When he began to descend and had a good grip on the ladder, Matt stepped forward. "Mr. Trueblood, I presume. I've been looking forward to meeting you."

Ten

Matt cocked his head, listening to the sound of light footsteps in the hall. "Libby? Come here a minute. We've got a visitor."

"A visitor? Who? I didn't hear the doorbell ring." Her voice grew clearer as she neared the doorway. "Matt, no one is supposed to be in here. You know that."

Libby swung through the door and came to a dead stop, her eyes widening in surprise as she took in the man on the ladder. "Eli? I mean, Mr. Trueblood?" She nudged Matt forward and edged around him, hurrying into the room. "You're not supposed to be back for another two weeks."

"Something tells me he's never been away." Matt moved beside her and they waited while the elderly man briskly climbed the rest of the way down the aluminum ladder. He folded it, leaned it tidily against the wall and walked over to a cluster of chairs. Sitting down, he motioned for Matt and Libby to join him.

Libby sat, unable to take her eyes off him. The inventor's appearance hadn't improved since the last time she'd seen him. He wore a shabby maroon sweat suit, purple socks and green running shoes. His shirt pocket bulged with papers and pencils. A shock of wiry gray hair stood on end all over his head, giving an observer the impression that he might have accidentally stuck his finger in an electric socket. His dark eyes, however, were bright with intelligence.

Folding her hands in her lap, Libby waited impatiently for the old man to collect his thoughts. She knew from experience that it wouldn't do a bit of good to rush him. She had liked Eli right from the beginning, had been a bit amused by his abstracted air and charmed by his kind eyes. Had even briefly felt sorry for him—imagining his lonely existence in the overwhelming house—until she'd realized that the inventor actually lived inside his head. As long as he had his thoughts and his work for company, he was a happy man.

Even so, holding a conversation with Eli had been a challenge. She and Carla had become so skilled in conducting homeowner interviews they could normally breeze through them in less than an hour. That had not been the case with Eli. Not only had the house been four times the normal size, but she'd had to pull him out of a deep mental fog each time she had a question about the house.

Finally, when neither of the men seemed anxious to begin, Libby couldn't wait any longer. "Is that right?" she prodded. "Have you been here all along, Mr. Trueblood?"

"Call me Eli," he said, nodding in answer to her question. "You've called me that for twelve days—no sense in changing now. Yes, yes, I've been here," he admitted with a rueful sigh. "I never left."

Libby's eyes narrowed as she gazed at him, her mood shifting from disbelief to anger. "Do you mean to say you've been wandering around the house watching us?"

Eli lifted a hand to slow her down. "I know you're upset, Libby. Maybe with cause. But let me say this first—I
never intruded on your privacy. I'm a scientist, not a voy-
eur."

She looked at him skeptically. "How could you not intrude?"

"I'll get back to that in a minute, if you don't mind."

"But—"

Eli looked at Matt, probably hoping for a more objective
listener. "I'm working on something fairly important right
now. Possibly it will end up with the government. And I
needed to run some critical tests. I also needed one or more
subjects for the tests I had developed."

"The walls that change colors?" Matt guessed.

Eli nodded. "I'm in the first phase of what will eventually be—if all goes well, that is—a mood equalizing system."

He shifted his glance from Matt to Libby and back again
as he spoke, selecting his words with great care. He was obviously not thrilled to be in a position where he felt obli-
gated to explain.

"It's based entirely on body heat. The colors of the lights
were simply an indication of your temperature and mood.
The object of the test, of course, was to chart as many
emotions as possible, as often as possible." His eyes spar-
kled briefly with scientific zeal. "This is just the first step,
you understand—testing, then collecting and analyzing the
data. The next phase will be to use the sensors in an oppos-
ing fashion."

"Science was never my strong point," Libby muttered,
leaning back in her chair.

"Think of the end result this way," Eli directed, his re-
luctance to disclose details apparently overcome by his en-
thusiasm to instruct. "If your temperature drops, possibly

indicating, say, depression, the sensors would trigger warm lights and try to neutralize the mood. Or if your temperature rose, cool lights could calm your mood. Of course, that part is a long way down the road."

"I don't know," she said, eyeing him doubtfully. "Some people might not want their moods altered."

"There is that, of course."

Matt whistled softly. "You know, you could have a real tiger by the tail on this one. I don't imagine drug companies will be thrilled to hear about a way to affect moods without medication."

"You're right," Eli said soberly. "And for that very reason, Jonas is the only one I've discussed this with until now. We're working on it together, you see. And I'd hate to have our work interrupted before we reach a satisfactory conclusion."

"Not to mention the fact that the two of you might be in danger," Matt added bluntly.

Eli briefly considered the possibility, then shook his head. "I doubt it. I've spend a lifetime inventing gadgets, and no one has ever been interested enough to threaten me."

"I'll bet you never took on an entire industry before, either," Matt commented.

"Matt's right," Libby said earnestly, scooting her chair closer to Eli's. "If this thing works, the drug companies could lose a big chunk of money, and they wouldn't be happy about that. Who knows what they'd do to stop you?"

Eli shrugged. "As I said, I haven't told anyone until now. But I believe I owe you an explanation, and I'm trusting you to be discreet. I'm trusting you, period."

"We won't say anything," Matt assured him, speaking for both of them. Gazing calmly at the inventor, he added, "So we've been your guinea pigs?"

Eli nodded. "So to speak. At first, when the need arose for testing, I didn't know how I'd get anyone in here unless they knew what I was doing. That wouldn't work, of course. Then I thought about getting house sitters. I saw the article in the paper about Sitting Pretty and it seemed a perfect solution."

"You were going to use *my* sitters?" Libby asked, not even trying to hide her annoyance. "I would never have put anyone in here if I'd known."

Eli shrugged. "It doesn't matter now. My idea didn't work out the way I expected it to. Your sitters were all busy, and you decided to come yourself. At first, I wondered if it was worth all the inconvenience to work with a single person, but I decided to try. As it was, even though I didn't have the lights fully working, I got some remarkable readings when you were in the room with your dog that first day." He turned to Matt. "And you were a definite bonus. Things perked up considerably once you moved in."

He appeared lost in thought for a few moments, then looked at Libby. "I said earlier that I didn't intrude on your privacy, and I didn't. I monitored the events in this room quite closely, but if anything of a private nature took place, I left my observation point. That's how you managed to short-circuit the system this afternoon," he added apologetically. "If I had stayed, I would have shut it down. You blew some of the bulbs, you know." His tone was more interested than accusing.

"What observation point?" Libby asked, ignoring the latter part of his statement. She was unable to decide if she was outraged or intrigued.

"There's a walkway behind that wall—" Eli gestured to the right "—with some holes in the carved woodwork that I can look through. Actually, there's an entire system of walkways throughout a good part of the house and enough room for me to work back there. Your dog often sensed me as I moved around. He wasn't happy about my presence and his reaction frightened you. I'm sorry about that."

"You scared the daylights out of me," Libby grumbled.

"I apologize," Eli said calmly, giving her an after-all-it's-for-science shrug.

"Have you been adjusting the program on the small robots?" Matt asked abruptly.

"Ah, the little robots." Eli gazed upward as if contemplating a beatific vision. "Yes. I spent more time on them than I had to spare, but as I watched you work with them I realized I could increase their capabilities to meet some of your commands. Each evening, I tweaked them up a little so they would respond to you better."

Libby eyed him with reluctant respect. "What did you do that made them react only to our voices?"

"Just the other night, I made voice tapes—one for each of you—and implanted them. Now the little guys respond to only three people—us."

Libby broke in again, remembering she had something to tell him and anxious to get the bad news over with. "Do you know about the break-in?"

He nodded. "I take full responsibility. You've been a good caretaker, so don't worry about it. By the way, I think I recognized the young man. I was working my way down to visit with Benson when I heard him making some noise in one of my offices. I watched him for some time from the walkway."

"What was he doing?" Matt asked with a frown.

"Searching for something," Eli said reluctantly. "Papers. He was going through my files. At any rate, I think he might be one of the window washers—the young one who had his hair covered by a baseball cap. This man's hair was long and all over the place, but he looked like the one who did all the outside work.''

Matt swore softly. ''You mean to say you knew he was in the house, and you didn't come out?''

''And ruin my entire setup with you two?'' He looked dumbfounded at the very thought. ''I didn't have anything worth stealing in there, and he wasn't doing any damage. Besides, I knew you would take care of things. You and Benson.'' He looked at Libby. ''And your admirable dog, of course.''

She returned his glance with a hopeful expression. ''You *did* commission the window washers to do the work, didn't you?''

Eli slowly shook his head. ''Unfortunately, no.'' He studied Libby's alarmed face and said quietly, ''But you acted most professionally. I can't fault your handling of the situation.''

Libby blinked. ''But then who sent them—and why?''

''An interesting question,'' Eli said thoughtfully. ''One that I've been mulling over. I don't know for sure, but if someone wanted to steal my notes on this program, it was a clever way to get into the house.''

''Good grief, it sounds like a bad movie.'' Libby looked at Matt and shook her head apologetically. ''And I thought you were overreacting.'' Turning back to Eli, she said, ''So why did you come out of hiding before the month was up?''

''I had to replace the bulbs that were blown out. I hadn't expected—'' He dug in his shirt pocket and pulled out a notepad and pencil, then scrawled a brief memo. Looking up, he murmured apologetically, ''I had to make a note to program the test for a more, ah, excessive range of emotions. At any rate, coming in here was a gamble, but the odds were in my favor. When it gets this late, you don't normally use this room. If you hadn't seen me, I would have continued the testing. Now, I'll have to stop, because your knowledge of the test would compromise the results. So, I'll just work with the information I have. Of course, I shall still pay for the entire month.''

"Well, I guess my sevices are no longer needed.'' Libby looked at her watch. "Good grief, it's almost ten. We should collect our things and leave. I can come back tomorrow and make a full report. That is, if you're going to be here. I—''

He held up a hand, stopping her in midspate. "There's no need for that. It's no time to be moving things. I'm going to be working tonight, just as I have since you arrived. You're welcome to stay, and you'll have the same privacy you've always had.'' That settled, he studied his note again, lost in reflection. When he looked up, he blinked as if surprised they were still there. "Oh, did I tell you I called Jonas earlier and asked him to come over with some additional data? We disagree on some of the calculations. He should be along in a few minutes.''

Matt sighed. "So he knew you were here all along. And I suppose he has a key to the place, too?''

"We're partners on this project. Of course. When he left the papers for me yesterday, he knew I'd come out and get them during the night. And if I had needed to see him, he would have used the secret entrance.''

"A secret entrance,'' Matt repeated with disgust. "I've never seen a house like this in all my life.'' In a quick change of subject, he asked, "Does Grant know about your project?''

"David? No, I didn't think that would be wise, even if he is Jonas's nephew.'' Eli stopped and glanced at his watch when the doorbell tolled gloomily through the house. "That should be Jonas now.''

Matt got up. "I'll get it.'' He left the room with Sam at his heels, his thoughts as bleak as the expression on the suit of armor he passed. He and Libby were supposed to have had two more weeks. Time to wipe away the past and build a future. Now, because of some exploding light bulbs, both the time and opportunity were gone. He would talk to her, he promised himself as he reached the door. Tonight, or early tomorrow. While they were still on neutral ground.

In the living room, Eli's dark eyes assessed the emotions on Libby's expressive face. "Will you forgive me for not being honest with you? If I had known any other way to do it, I would have."

"That's all right, Eli." Murmuring automatically, she tilted her head and listened to the flurry of voices at the door. Her thoughts weren't nearly as comforting as her words.

Leaving.

Tomorrow.

She and Matt hadn't even had one full day of their grace period.

"Ah, Matt, there you are," she heard Jonas say vaguely as he walked into the house. "Sorry to bother you, but I—"

"Jonas. Grant." Matt's voice was abrupt.

"Evening, Flint. Uncle Jonas doesn't like to drive at night, so I came along."

"I have some more calculations for Eli," Jonas said, pulling a crumpled sheaf from his pocket. "If I could just leave them on his—"

"Jonas?" Eli hastened to the living room door and waved to his partner. "In here."

"Ah, Eli, you're back." Jonas surged ahead of the others, straightening the papers in a futile attempt to remove the creases. David lagged behind Matt, with Sam walking stiff-legged at a distance beside him.

The two older men wasted no time on greetings. They walked over to the wall by the ladder, already engrossed in their discussion. Eli touched a section of the carved wood and Libby watched in astonishment as a door slid open in the paneling.

She rose to greet David and her eyes widened even more when he slid a gun from his jacket pocket. He motioned for her to be silent and trained the gun on Matt's back.

"Eli, Uncle Jonas, I'm afraid I need those papers. All of them. Right now." David kept his gaze on Matt while he spoke. "No, don't try to be a hero," he added when Matt turned around to face him. "I just want the papers and no one will get hurt. Don't move," he warned him, motioning for Libby to come closer. "My men will be here in a few minutes. The window washers," he added with a faint smile.

Over by the wall, the two inventors were oblivious to the drama taking place just a few yards away. Eli frowned at his partner and shook his head. "No, Jonas, that can't be right. Look, I'll show you." He stepped through the opening, closely followed by Jonas, and the door slid closed behind them.

"Uncle Jonas! Eli!" At the panic in David's voice, Libby stiffened. Matt, she noted with disgust, looked relaxed and only mildly curious.

"Why window washers?" he asked calmly, a thread of genuine curiosity in his voice.

David shot a look of frustration at the sealed door. "Why not? They were referred to me when I let it be known in certain quarters that I needed some men with a talent for burglary and few scruples. It seems they've had a small side business going for some time, checking out homes while they clean the windows, then going back to visit after dark. In this case, all they had to do was pretend that Eli had hired them to come out."

"But why?" Libby burst out. "What on earth could make you rob your own uncle and his best friend? You already seem to have everything going for you."

"*Seem* is the operative word here." David waggled the gun from Matt to Libby. "We might as well sit down. Carefully. We're going to wait until they come out."

He backed up, waiting while Libby dropped into an overstuffed love seat and Matt took a straight-backed chair near her. Sam whined anxiously and stood between them. David sat a few feet away, keeping his gun trained on Matt.

"I picked a bad location for my development," he finally said. "I bought the property for a song. That should have warned me, but I thought I had pulled off a slick deal. They're putting in a dump less than a mile away from the development. Now, the people who have money won't even look at the houses, and the people who are looking can't afford them.

"With enough cash, I can pay off some people and get the dump moved. Without it, I'm sunk. It's that simple."

"Simple?" Libby looked at him in disbelief. "You call robbing Eli and Jonas *simple?*"

"Who's going to pay you?" Matt asked.

David shifted in his chair and looked at them defiantly. "I have a buyer. I overheard Eli and Jonas talking one day, and I mentioned the project to someone I know, just in casual conversation. Next thing I knew, someone was offering some big bucks to 'acquire' the necessary information." He shrugged. "I couldn't turn it down."

"David, why don't you forget it?" Libby's voice was soft. "Just put away the gun, tell the men you've changed your mind and we'll forget this ever happened."

He shook his head. "I can't. I've already taken a chunk of money from these guys."

"But you'll never get away with it."

He looked at her consideringly. Flashing a smile, he said, "I'm betting that you're wrong. I don't think either of the old guys will turn me in. And, hell, those eggheads have so many ideas in the works, they'll move on to the next one without even missing a beat."

"And what if they start all over with this one?" Matt asked coolly. "I suspect that the guys who gave you the money would apply some muscle next—both to you and the old men—to be sure their work goes *real* slow."

"I don't think so."

"Think again, then. People like that always get their money's worth."

Matt's blunt words rattled David, and when he jumped to his feet, Sam leaped, his teeth closing on the cuffs of David's pants. Matt dived for the gun and Libby watched in horror as the two men fell to the floor, rolling and knocking aside the furniture. Matt's hand gripped David's wrist, forcing it over his head. With a deafening roar, the gun discharged.

"Matt? *Matt.* Are you hurt? Answer me, damn it!" Ears ringing, Libby climbed over an upended table to get closer and answered her own question. There was no blood and both men were still fighting for the gun.

"The lights," Matt gritted, bending David's wrist back. "Get the lights!"

Lights? The man was in a fight for his life and he was worried about lights? Libby blinked. Omigod. The other men. David's men. The window washers. They'd be drawn by the sound of gunfire and Matt wouldn't stand a chance with a crowd like that.

She dashed to the door and looked despairingly at all the lights blazing in the hall and entryway. When her gaze fell on the motionless suit of armor across the hall, she remembered the tasks Matt had assigned the smaller robots. She clapped her hands, and within seconds, the whiz kids were lined up before her.

"The lights," she gasped. "Turn off the lights. All of them. In the whole house. For God's sake, hurry! Go!"

When they bustled away, she reached in and hit the switch by the door just as Matt tore the gun from David's hand and tossed it aside. He told Sam, who was still snarling and tugging David's cuffs, to sit.

David dug his elbow in Matt's ribs, broke away and stumbled toward the door. Fleeing past Libby into the pitch-black hall, he knocked her to the floor. As she picked herself up, Matt swore and lunged after him, running straight into her.

"Matt! It's me!" Libby's cry was cut off and Matt grunted, twisting to take the brunt of the impact as they fell.

"Damn it, Libby, can't you stay out of trouble?" he demanded unreasonably as he pulled her to her feet. "Get back in there and get David's gun, then shoot any bastard that comes through the door. I'll call out when I come back. If you're in any doubt if it's me, don't shoot. Sam, stay!"

He gave her a hug and was gone before she could tell him that aside from playing with a cap pistol as a child, she'd never even held a gun. She hadn't the foggiest idea how to shoot one.

Nevertheless, she crawled across the floor in the dark, running her hands across the lumpy carpet, deciding that she could at least keep someone else from finding it. When her hand finally settled on the cold steel, she gave a gusty sigh of relief. She placed the gun by her side and sat cross-legged on the floor, petting Sam and considering her options.

She could alert Eli and Jonas—that is, she could if she knew how to open the sliding door. She shook her head in disgust. No, they were so engrossed in their calculations, they wouldn't hear her if she broke down the door with a battering ram. So that was out.

And moving from this room would be foolish, even though she didn't relish the idea of wimpily waiting while Matt crept through the house chasing robbers and potential murderers. But since he knew both the layout of the house and the paths taken by the robots, he'd be safer and more effective if she kept out of the way. Besides, she admitted gloomily, there wasn't a single thing she could do out there that he couldn't do better and faster.

When a startled, masculine shriek echoed down the hall, Libby snatched the gun, placing her finger firmly on the trigger. With her other hand, she held on to Sam.

The minutes seemed like hours. It was easy for Matt to tell her to wait, she thought, disgruntled. He was out there doing something, not sitting like a lump in a dark room. On the other hand, she reminded herself, he not only knew what needed doing, he knew how to do it. So she sat, clutching the gun and Sam, considering the merits of taking up karate.

"Libby? Liiibby?"

The eerie whisper drifting through the room scared her out of her wits. It also proved to her that she did know how to shoot a gun. The bullet slammed into the ceiling and the sound deafened her for a second time. When her ears stopped ringing, she heard the whisper again, only this time it was ruffled.

"Hey! Hold your fire! It's me. Benson. I called the police and they should be here any minute. Oh, and I ran into Matt out there. He's fine. Having a helluva time. There are four guys out there, plus the fool nephew."

He chuckled. "Did you hear that yelp a while ago? One of the big robots cornered one of the window cleaners. Scared the hell out of him. Between Matt and the big guys, there are three down, two to go. I'm going back out there to help him. See you in a few minutes. Damn! I haven't had this much fun in a long time.''

As quickly as he'd arrived, Benson was gone, leaving Libby sitting in the dark, cursing herself for being an idiot. She hadn't even thought of calling the police.

Three hours later, the same two officers who had been there before, plus reinforcements, shepherded their five prisoners out the door.

Jonas watched them go, shaking his head. "I'm sorry, Eli. I had no idea David's real estate venture was in trouble. I would have helped him if he'd asked.''

"I know. I would have, too.''

"Do you suppose we should follow them down to the station?''

Eli shook his head. "No, I think a night or three in a cell will do a world of good for David.''

Jonas dropped into the chair next to Benson. "They want us to go down tomorrow and press charges,'' he reminded Eli.

"I know.''

"Should we?''

"I don't know,'' Eli admitted with a sigh.

Benson got up and poured five glasses of brandy. After he handed them around, he said, "It might just be the making of that nephew of yours if you do file charges. Nothing happened and no one was hurt. He'd probably get off with a suspended sentence, maybe some community service. And it would give the cops a chance to close down the window-cleaning business. What do you think, Matt?''

"I think you're right.'' Matt's voice was crisp and succinct. Whatever the old men did, he thought disgustedly, David Grant wouldn't get what he deserved. Matt cheered himself with the thought that whoever had hired David would probably send someone to take their money out of his hide.

Libby watched the two scientists, her eyes soft with sympathy. They had strolled out from behind the sliding door just as Benson was letting in the police, and Matt was—with David's gun out of her hand and firmly in his—escorting the five men toward the front door.

The four window cleaners hadn't said a word beyond demanding a lawyer. David, on the other hand, had been quite vocal. Even so, it had taken some time for the old men to believe that not only was David involved, he was also the ringleader.

Eleven

A few minutes later, Matt turned to Libby and caught her in the middle of a yawn. "I think we've all just about had it," he said decisively to the others. "Thanks for the invitation to spend the night, Eli. We'll straighten this place up in the morning." He tugged Libby to her feet and nodded to the three men. "Good night. Try to get some sleep."

Once in their room, he flipped the spread to the foot of the bed before turning to Libby and tugging her shirt over her head. Hoping she was as tired as he was and that she'd wait for their talk until morning, he said, "Come on, sweetheart, you need to hit the sack."

She looked at him groggily when he put his hands on her shoulders and gently pushed until she was sitting on the mattress. Settling against the pillow, she yawned and mumbled, "I don't know what's the matter with me. I was fine until just a few minutes ago."

"It's all that adrenaline. You topped out and now you've crashed. You'll feel better in the morning."

She yawned again. "Are you sure?"

"Positive. Trust me." He shed his clothes and crawled in beside her, wrapping his arm around her and pulling her close.

His heart jolted when she curled against him. She didn't do it provocatively. Nor enticingly. She was just soft with trust and fatigue. In a few seconds, she would drift off, staying close during the night, as if she needed his presence, his warmth, in order to sleep.

As if she needed him.

He savored the thought for a moment. He couldn't remember the time when someone had needed him for anything other than a school or business project. Even Caroline. She had wanted him—at first—but she had never needed him.

"I'm going to be tied up with Eli a good part of the day," he murmured, brushing his lips across her cheek. "He wants to change the circuit that his robots make in the halls. When we're through, I'll help you pack and move your office." Libby nodded and he felt her muscles gradually relax. She gave a deep sigh and slept.

For several hours, Matt held Libby close and stared into the darkness, trying to hold off the dawn. He didn't want to sleep. He just wanted to feel Libby against him, listen to the sound of her soft breathing. When he thought of the next day, that his life might go to hell in a hand basket in a matter of minutes, he needed her warmth far more than she needed his.

Early the next morning, Matt felt Libby's hair slide across his shoulder and instinctively his hand trailed down to the curve of her bottom. There couldn't be a better way to start

a day, he reflected lazily. They had come through last night's
brouhaha with their skins intact, and Libby was in his arms,
her breasts pressed against his chest and one of her legs
tucked between his. Yeah, it had all the makings of a great
day. Then he remembered what they had ahead of them and
his muscles tightened.

They were going to talk.

And the outcome of that discussion could change his
whole world. *Would* change it. He would either end up back
in the cold, lonely hell he'd endured for the past six months
or start a new life, complete with Libby's laughter and
warmth . . . and unconditional love.

Talking wasn't the problem, he thought bleakly. Dissem-
inating information was part of his job. His presentations
to potential clients were normally informative and flawless.
He was frequently asked to speak at seminars on topics
ranging from plant security to computer theft. With his experience and knowledge, he could have done most of them
in his sleep. The fact that he had more offers than he could
accept was proof that he had the ability to communicate.

So, *talking* wasn't the problem. It was the things they were
going to discuss that had him in a cold sweat. He just wasn't
any good at laying his feelings on the line. Hell, his track
record made that clear enough.

As a child, he had openly asked for love, demanded it
from his career-driven parents. What he had been given was
care from a series of housekeepers. As a teen, proud and
vulnerable, still aching for the approval of his parents, he
had set out to excel both academically and in sports. When
he'd brought home one trophy after another, he had silently added it to his growing collection, knowing his parents would never even notice.

Somehow, he'd thought marriage with Caroline would
change things. It didn't. He hadn't counted on marrying a

woman who knew as little about love as he did, one who made the same mistake he had—thinking that good sex was love. By the time they had agreed to get a divorce, there was nothing good left between them. When she had blamed him for the fiasco, told him he didn't know how to make a woman happy, he hadn't argued. Hell, what could he say? As far as he knew, he'd never made *anyone* happy.

Except Libby. For five months.

When Libby sighed and snuggled closer to him, murmuring something soft and sleepy, Matt's body tightened. He bent to kiss her shoulder and he felt her lips move in a smile against his chest.

"Libby?"

"Mmm?"

"Are you awake?"

"Uh-uh."

In spite of his worry, Matt grinned. She was the only woman in the world who could be nine-tenths asleep and still drive him crazy. Her fingertips were like delicate butterfly kisses, settling here, there, gliding over him in a random pattern that had his nerve endings screaming.

When he touched the tip of her breast with a gentle finger, she caught her breath and moved restlessly against him. His mouth closed over the tight bead, and Libby laced her fingers through his hair, holding him close against her.

"Matt?" The murmured word was perilously close to a purr.

"Mmm?"

"I want you."

He brushed her nipple with his tongue and felt her stiffen. His hand blazed a path down her belly, through the triangle of hair, and he smiled. She did want him. And she was ready. Right now.

Libby lifted her hips against his hand, inviting him as women had done with their men for centuries, mutely, urging him to accept what she was offering. And when Matt slid into her she wrapped herself around him, holding him close, closer, until she felt his heart beating against her.

His hard body pressed her into the mattress and he moved within her, again and again, until she shuddered and cried out, whispering his name over and over in a mindless, sensual chant.

Afterward, Matt held her, waiting for his heartbeat to slow, watching her fall back to sleep in his arms, knowing that if the world ended in the next moment, he would die a happy man.

Much later, Matt looked at his watch and winced. Eli would be waiting for him. He kissed Libby's smooth shoulder and eased out of bed, covering her carefully so the cool morning air wouldn't wake her. It took him only a couple of minutes to dress and shave.

When he opened the bedroom door, Eli was already at the far end of the hall, examining one of the large robots that had been disconnected. Matt sighed. He recognized the look of a man raring to go, a man who ignored ordinary things—like breakfast. "Mornin', Eli."

"Mmm-hmm." Eli looked up from where he sat on the floor. "You did good work on this."

"Thanks. Troubleshooters learn all kinds of handy things." Matt ambled past him, heading for the kitchen.

Eli peered inside the robot's leg at a small electronic coil. "Come here and look at this for a minute."

Matt kept walking. Looking over his shoulder, he said, "After breakfast."

"I think you'll find it very interesting."

"I wouldn't be a bit surprised," Matt said, not stopping. "Everything you do is interesting, but I have a firm policy to get coffee and food in my stomach before I tackle a job. Any job.''

As he expected, Eli followed him, tucking a sheaf of papers under his arm. He sat at the table and pulled out several diagrams while Matt poured coffee and collected granola, milk and muffins. "Have you eaten?"

Eli blinked at him, his dark eyes hazy with thought. "What?"

"Eaten," Matt repeated, setting a bowl in front of the inventor. "Food."

"Hmm." Eli stared thoughtfully at the muffins. "I don't remember."

"Fine. Have some breakfast." Matt poured some granola in his bowl and pushed the rest across the table, doing the same with the milk and muffins. It was no time to worry about simple courtesies, he decided. Eli was apt to turn a page and get lost in his papers again, so there was no sense in waiting for him to serve himself first. "Is Benson still around?"

Eli nodded. "He's decided to stay on for a couple of days."

"What have you decided to do about Grant?"

"David?" Thoughtfully, Eli turned his steaming mug of coffee by the handle. "Benson sat with us for a while last night and went into more detail about how we might be able to make a deal with the police—press charges so they can go after the window washers, but negotiate for a more lenient sentence for David." He looked up to see if the plan impressed Matt.

When he couldn't read Matt's expression, he shrugged and said, "After all, David only *tried*. He didn't actually take anything. And I don't really think he wanted to. Things got out of hand, and he just—

"Got in over his head?" Matt bit into his blueberry muffin and leaned back, waiting. He partially agreed with the old man. He thought Grant was weak rather than criminal, inclined to look for the easy way out. He also thought that somewhere down the road, if Grant got in financial hot water again, he'd do exactly the same thing he tried last night.

"Precisely." Eli nodded as if trying to convince himself. "He got in over his head. What do you think of our plan?"

Matt shrugged. "It seems fair."

The older man gazed at him for several long moments. "I think I hear a but in there. What?"

"I wouldn't make it too easy on him," Matt said bluntly. "In fact, I'd put the fear of God in him before I let him find out he didn't have to do time." He took another bite of his muffin and munched thoughtfully. "If you and Jonas have the money, it might be worth your while to help him get settled somewhere else—far away from you. If he drags his feet at the idea, you could always mention that his 'buyer' might be sending someone to get back their money. One way or another."

Eli brightened. "That's not a bad idea."

"Is Benson going to the police with you?"

His mouth full of muffin, Eli nodded. Swallowing, he said thickly, "That's why he's staying on for a few days."

"Good." The two old men couldn't have a better mentor, Matt reflected. He had a feeling that Benson, with his good-old-boy routine, could outthink and outtalk any of the legal talent the cops could come up with.

Eli looked at Matt's empty bowl. "Are you done? Can we get to work now?"

"In a minute." Matt took the dishes over to the sink. "Libby laid down the housekeeping rules the day I arrived here. I clean up after myself." He rinsed the dishes in hot water and dried them. Putting away the towel, he said to Eli, "Okay, let's go."

Eli got up, tucking his papers under his arm. "What do you want to do first?"

Matt grinned. "I want to see your work space behind the walls. But before that, I want to see how your sliding panel works."

Libby turned over in bed, reaching for Matt. Instead of touching his warm skin, her hand slid across the cool sheet. A quick glance at her watch jerked her upright. By now, he had been up for several hours and was undoubtedly toiling away with Eli, tightening up the robots' sentry areas.

Thinking of Matt inevitably turned her mind to their forthcoming discussion. It wasn't going to be easy—especially for a man who had been trained by experts to be closemouthed. She had given the matter of his skillful evasion a great deal of thought in the last day or so, considered the little he had to say about his family and ex-wife. It was as if he had closed a door on those years, as if they had no bearing on his present life.

But he was dead wrong, she reflected, heading for the shower. Whatever had happened to him during those years was definitely affecting them now—and she was just the person to tell him so.

Matt had never once said he loved her.

What he *had* said more times than she could count was that he needed her, wanted her. Odd, she thought, lathering her hair, when they had been together she had never missed the words, had never even noticed that they weren't there.

But then, maybe it wasn't so odd, she decided, tilting her head and letting the water rinse away the shampoo. Matt had been the friend and lover she'd always dreamed of finding. His presence in her house had added a vital force to her life, an energy she hadn't even realized was lacking. The gleam of hunger in his eyes, the approval in his voice, the touch of his hands, the heat of his body had shown her all she needed to know. It was no wonder she hadn't missed the words.

But they were important, those missing words. Necessary. She gave the faucet handles a brisk turn and stepped out of the shower. You knew exactly where you stood when you had the words.

Libby reached for the towel, then stopped, her hand frozen in midair. How many times had she said "I love you" to Matt? she wondered, staring blankly at the piled fabric. Often enough so he believed it? She winced and took the towel, slowly drying herself.

Maybe not.

The only times she had told him were when they were actually making love. True, the number was somewhere near astronomical, but perhaps a man who was gun-shy, who had reasons to doubt, would rationalize that the words, coming at that time, were simply a part of a shattering experience.

Could a man possibly be that dense, she wondered, stepping into clean shorts and turning to grab a shirt from the closet.

Yes. He could.

After stripping the sheets and remaking the bed, Libby pulled out her suitcase. It took only a few minutes to toss her clothes in and collect her things from the bathroom.

Still pondering the density of some men, she ate a quick breakfast and tidied the kitchen. She entered her office just in time to answer the telephone.

"Libby? Guess what?"

Grinning at her cousin's enthusiastic question, she dropped into her chair by the desk. "I give. What?"

"You should see the terrific résumés we're getting in answer to our ad! There are more adventurous secretaries out there than I thought."

"Why shouldn't there be? We'll be terrific employers."

"Yeah, but they don't know that, and we listed ourselves as 'small but growing.' That usually means the pay is peanuts. I mean it, these women sound fantastic."

"If they're that great, maybe we should call the one we hire an administrative assistant."

"Hmm. Not a bad idea," Carla said thoughtfully. "Not bad at all. Listen, check your calendar, will you? What do you have on tap when you leave Eli's? I want to get some of these gals scheduled for interviews as soon as possible."

"Is tomorrow soon enough?" Libby asked dryly, propping her feet on the table. She could almost hear her cousin thinking on the other end of the line.

"What happened?" Carla finally asked in a voice of doom. "Please don't tell me the house burned down. My heart couldn't stand it."

"Relax, Cuz. Eli's back. No, I guess that isn't the right word, because he never left. At any rate, we walked into the living room last night, and there he was."

"What?" Carla shrieked. "You mean he's been creeping around the house all the time you were there? Are you all right? Don't move a muscle. I'm coming right over and I'll have a few things to say to the old lecher. Just—"

"Of course," Libby added blandly, "that was before five men broke into the house and tried to rob us at gunpoint."

"What?"

"And Eli, along with a friend, disappeared behind some secret sliding doors."

"My God."

"And Matt and the robots captured them all."

"Is there anything else?" Carla moaned.

"Uh, yeah. I shot a hole in the ceiling with the robber's gun."

"Oh, hell."

"But Eli said not to worry. He's very satisfied with the way I handled things."

"He should be, the little creep. He's been getting his jollies sneaking peeks at you."

Libby's laughter drowned out the rest of Carla's muttering. "Carla, relax. It's okay. Really."

"Libby, I'm going to throttle you. You mean you've been making this up? None of it really happened?"

Libby wiped her eyes. "All of it happened," she said cheerfully. "Listen, it's a long story, and I've got to get this office stuff moved out of here. I'll tell you when I get back to the house. Matt said he'd help me, but he's playing mad scientist with Eli right now, and there's no telling when he'll be through. I don't feel like sitting around here all day waiting for him."

"I've got a better idea," Carla said. "I'll come over and help you, and you can talk while we pack."

"Terrific. And we'll have one last cup of Eli's coffee."

It was dusk when Matt walked out of Eli's littered work area behind the walls. He felt the difference in the house immediately.

Libby was gone.

The cold that seeped into his bones was an old familiar feeling. He had lived with it most of his life. In fact, he hadn't even known he was cold until he moved in with Libby and had been enveloped in the warmth of her life, her arms.

The office, minus her equipment and neatly converted back into a spare room, and the empty bedroom only confirmed what he already knew. He looked around for a note, knowing there would be none.

When Eli returns, it'll be time to face the real world. We'll go to my house and talk.

Panic shot through him, leaving a gnawing pain in his stomach. She would be waiting, and he still didn't know what to say. She needed to be healed once and for all, and he didn't know if he could do it. She needed a man who would keep her happy for a lifetime, and he didn't know if he was that man.

Throwing his clothes into the duffel bag, he swore. They were supposed to have two more weeks before they reached this point—time they would have used to build a bridge to the future.

Thirteen days, mostly spent apart, hadn't been long enough.

It...just...hadn't...been...long...enough.

Libby sat in the dark on the screened porch at the back of her house, listening to the crickets and waiting. In the distance, she could hear the occasional honk of a car horn and the screech of brakes. Since she had arrived home, she had aired out the house, watered the plants, fixed dinner for herself and Sam, showered, washed her hair again and optimistically changed the sheets on the bed.

Matt would come, she knew. It might be tonight, tomorrow or the next day, but he would come. He wouldn't walk away this time, at least not without talking to her first. She lay on the daybed, looking at the stars overhead, trying to quiet her pounding heart and relax her knotted muscles.

Matt would come.

It seemed hours later that she heard the creak of the side gate, the soft sound as he brushed by the tall plants on his way to her.

"Libby?" His voice was hushed.

"In here." She rose, opened the screen door and walked into his arms. "I've been waiting."

"I was with Eli until just a few minutes ago. I threw my stuff in my bag and got here as soon as I could."

She looked down at his side. "Your bag?"

"It's in the car."

Wincing at his controlled voice, she said, "I knew you'd come."

Matt ran his hand down her body. She was wearing shorts again, but the night air had cooled and she was chilled. He scooped her up and carried her to the daybed, settling her in his lap, his arms tightening convulsively around her. "Oh, God, Libby. Do you know how much I love you?"

She nodded, her head rubbing against his shoulder, barely able to breathe for the joy and pain in her chest. "Yes. Every bit as much as I love you." And she did know, she realized. Somehow, she had always known. And knowing, had been even more wounded when he'd left. Her fingers gently touched his cheek. "But you've never said that before."

"Just one indication of my thickheadedness," he said tightly.

Her hand slid around his neck, holding him as if she'd never let him go. "But... telling me isn't enough, Matt. There has to be more. There has to be trust." She took a steadying breath. "You loved me before, didn't you?"

He stiffened. "That's a hell of a question. You know I did!"

"I hoped you did." She hesitated, then plunged in. "But you left me anyway. So before I open myself up to that kind of pain again, I want to know why. I want to know that it won't happen again."

He shifted and her fingers clutched at the open neck of his shirt, as if to keep him where he was, to keep him holding her. "Oh, hell, Libby, I just thought you'd be happier with someone else. I told you that."

"I know you did. I want to know why. Did I ever give you the impression that I wasn't happy with you?"

He shook his head. "Never, not for a second." He hesitated, then added, "No, not really."

"What do you mean, 'not really.'"

He gave a sharp sigh. "The last few weeks, I thought you were in love with Trent."

"*Jason?* Matt, how could you?"

"I was crazy jealous, that's how. Every word that came out of your mouth was Jason this and Jason that. At the time, it was real easy to think it."

"That was it? You left because of Jason?" Matt started to get up, but she held on until he settled back against the pillows, his arms tightening around her. "Or was there something else, someone else that made you think I'd be better off without you?"

The silence seemed to last forever. Finally, he swore softly and ran a hand through his hair. "Libby, I'm no damn good talking about the past. It's over and done with, and it doesn't do any good to dredge things up."

She studied his closed expression by the gleam of moonlight shafting through the screen. "What things? I can't think of anything that happened while we were together that's so hard to talk about. Wait a minute," she said slowly, feeling her way. "You're not talking about us, are you?"

"No." He shifted beneath her. "Libby, this is stupid. It just doesn't do any good to rehash this stuff."

"We're going to do it anyway." *What* stuff? she wondered anxiously. Taking a stab in the dark, she said softly, "How far back are we going here, Matt? Six months? Six years? Twenty years?" When he didn't answer, she took a deep breath. "Okay, Matt, if it takes all night, it takes all night."

Settling more firmly in his lap, she said casually, "You've never told me much about your family. As long as we've got the rest of the night—the rest of the month, actually—I'd like to hear about them." When he stiffened, she wrapped her arms around his neck, knowing instinctively that the next few minutes weren't going to be easy. "What were your folks like?"

He shrugged, finally saying in a colorless voice, "They took care of me, gave me what I needed."

Well, that said a whole world, she thought with a sigh, thinking of the love and support she'd received from her family. They had been, and still were, everything a family should be—noisy, boisterous, offering commiseration or a nudge in the right direction when she needed it.

"So you got what you needed," she prodded gently. "Did you get what you wanted?"

He shrugged again. "The subject never came up. Fact of the matter is, *I* never came up—to their expectations."

"What did they want?" she demanded, rearing back to look at him in astonishment. "You were an honor student, president of the class and an outstanding athlete. They should have been popping their buttons with pride. What else did they want from you?"

"I don't know." His voice was controlled. "I never did."

She sat up, turning until she straddled his thighs. Looking him in the eye, she said, "Well, *I* know something. They didn't deserve you."

Beneath her anger, she wanted to weep. Then, imagining a young boy bringing home his trophies, hoping for acceptance and never getting it, she also wanted to strangle those people.

"It was their loss," she told him, touching his mustache with a gentle finger. "They never knew what they had."

She leaned against him, just reminding him that she was there. "How about now?" she asked hopefully. "Things do change. They must be very proud of you."

Matt looked over her shoulder into the darkness. "They live in the east. I haven't seen them for several years. I call them on birthdays and holidays."

"That's nice," she said inadequately. She kissed his cheek softly, trying to erase the legacy of pain left by people who did not know how to love. Taking a shaky breath, she said briskly, "Okay, so after college you worked for the military-slash-government, got married, got divorced and built a successful business of your own. Right?"

He nodded, sounding relieved. "Right."

Libby leaned her cheek against his shoulder. So who else's ghost are we fighting here? she wondered. Well, she had opened this particular can of worms and she'd see it through to the end, come hell or high water!

"Matt?" Her voice was deceptively soft.

"Hmm?"

"Will you tell me about your ex-wife?" She felt his sudden tension and knew she had hit the jackpot. "What's she like?"

"Libby, this is really stupid."

"Humor me, okay? What's she like? Were the two of you ever happy?"

"We shouldn't have gotten married," he said brusquely, goaded to reply. "Neither one of us knew a damn thing about love. I couldn't make her happy. She told me I wouldn't do any better with you."

Libby blinked. "This is the woman you told me was out of your life and no concern of ours? The one who was long gone and forgotten?" When he nodded, she took an enraged breath. "Wait just a minute here. The way I see it, when someone is out of your life, you don't see them, you don't hear from them. Do I understand that she still calls you?"

His fingers touched her hair. "Not anymore."

"How in the hell could she convince you that I wasn't happy with you?" she demanded furiously, ignoring his quick response. "She's never even met me!"

For the first time in a long time, Matt saw a glimmer of hope. Libby wasn't backing away, she wasn't shocked, she wasn't buying into one word he was saying. And she didn't seem to think he lacked anything. She was just fighting mad, ready to slay all the dragons in their lives. He was beginning to feel like the fool of the century, but he was going to get this behind them, once and for all.

He shaped her face with his hands and met her angry gaze. "Her parting shot at our divorce was that while I was a decent lover, I didn't know the first thing about making a woman happy. And even less about keeping her that way."

Libby blinked, rage rushing through her so quickly she felt dizzy. "And you believed her?" she asked, astonished. "She said that *once,* and you carried it around with you for years?"

He grimaced. "When she didn't have anything else to do, she'd call me up and remind me, just in case I had forgotten, in case I was making some woman miserable. That way, I'd know *why* she was miserable. She called me a couple of days before I walked out on you."

"Well, damn you, Matt," Libby said with gathering fury. She whacked him on the chest with the side of her fist, and then did it again. Tears rolled down her cheeks. "That's it? Some stupid, insecure, vindictive woman tries to cover up her own inadequacies by blaming you, and for *that* you ruin my life? You blockhead!"

Impatiently pushing aside the hair that had fallen forward over her eyes, she said, "You listen to me. If you ever make me unhappy, *I'll* tell you, damn it. Me! Not your parents, not your ex-wife, not anybody! Me! Do you understand? Me!"

She whacked him on the chest again for good measure. "Until then, I expect you to believe I'm happy. I expect you to trust me enough to talk to me. And I never expect you to walk out that door again unless you intend to come back. Do you hear that?" Her voice rose until she was shouting at him.

Matt grabbed her, rolling over until he was on top of her, loving her temper, her fury. Loving her, with all his heart and soul. "I imagine everyone in the neighborhood hears you," he said in a voice shaky with relief and laughter. Then grabbing her hands and securing them over her head, he asked, "Does that mean I can stay?"

Libby softened, going boneless beneath him. "It means you *will* stay, even if I have to learn how to shoot a gun to keep you here."

She tugged her hands free and wrapped her arms around his neck, pressing against him until they rolled on their sides. "Oh, Matt, I've been so scared."

He sighed, resting his head next to hers. "Me, too. I've done nothing but make and break resolutions ever since I walked through Eli's door. I told myself I wouldn't touch you, wouldn't push you, that I'd give you all the time you needed, then I got you in my arms and all hell broke loose. After I let you go, I'd start all over again, promising to be patient." He looked at her ruefully. "But my patience never lasted very long."

The smile in her eyes was one any woman would understand. "It was the only thing that made me hopeful," she admitted. "I didn't have much else to cling to." She tightened her arms until her lips were only a whisper away from his. He dipped his head and the kiss that began as a tender renewal sparked and exploded, leaving them panting and clinging to each other.

When she could talk again, she looked up at him. "Why didn't you tell me any of this before?"

"I couldn't," Matt said simply, holding her as if he'd never let her go. "I didn't know how. I've never talked to anyone about how I felt. I had shut my feelings away for so long, I didn't even think about them. Much. I just...did what had to be done. When I moved in here with you, I hoped like hell it would be permanent, but I never believed for a minute that it would be. And then you started coming home from work every day talking about another man." He felt the jolt run through her.

"Matt!" She stretched the word into a long groan. "Couldn't you tell frustration and exasperation from I've-found-a-new-man-and-I'd-please-like-you-to-pack-your-bags?"

"No."

The simple word shook her heart, and broke it a little, for the boy who, despite a sterile childhood, had grown into a man of enormous passion, a man who had just now learned to trust someone with what was in his heart.

"I love you, Matthew Flint," she whispered, brushing dampness away from his eyes. "I have since the day I met you, and I will till the day I die."

Matt gave her one last chance. "Are you sure?" She didn't take it. Her kiss told him positively that she didn't want it. Would never want it.

"I'm positive." Then, remembering what he had said earlier, Libby prodded him with a slim finger. "Why doesn't your ex call anymore?" she demanded.

Matt's gaze became grim and held more than a tinge of self-disgust. Tightening his arms around her, he said, "Because while walking out on you was an all-time high in stupidity, it gave me plenty of time to think about things I've done—and haven't done. I knew I was no more responsible for the breakup of my marriage than Caroline was, but I'd put up with her version of the story because I didn't care enough to argue about it."

He shrugged. "I figured my shoulders were broad and that her accusations couldn't hurt me. But after I left you, I realized I was wrong—her poison was touching us. So I made my first and last call to her since we broke up." He touched her cheek with a gently finger. "I promise, she's out of our lives. Okay?"

"Okay." She rested her head on his shoulder, the tension gradually easing from her body. Suddenly, she stiffened and said, "Oh, no!"

"What?" His gut tightened. Damn it, he'd known it couldn't be as easy as that! *"What?"*

"Your business," she wailed softly. "You've just gotten established in Phoenix, and I can't leave here. Carla and I are doing so well. We have such plans. I can't back out on her, Matt, I just can't."

He exhaled slowly. "Libby," he said through gritted teeth, "don't ever, *ever* do that to me again. I'll move the damn business back here. It's no big deal." He held her tighter. "Now just let me hold you, okay? No more shocks, no more tears, just let me hold you."

Libby sighed, in full agreement, relaxing for the first time in days. Later, they would make love. Later, they would talk more, exorcise all the ghosts. Later, they would do everything that needed doing, but for now they just needed to hold and be held. To know that what they had was forever.

A long time later, she blinked up at him like a curious, green-eyed kitten. "How did you know I was staying at Eli's?"

Matt dropped a kiss on the tip of her nose, thinking fast. "I'll tell on our fifth anniversary," he promised. When she narrowed her eyes, he said, "Make it the tenth."

Ten was a nice safe number, he decided. If he was lucky, she'd forget all about it before then. Telling her that he'd paid a couple to interview as house sitters would definitely not please her. Explaining that once she had hired them, they had agreed to let him know if Libby ever needed his help would most certainly annoy her. The fact that they'd refused to sit in Trueblood's house, overheard her tell Carla she would stay there and called him with the news was not something he wanted to discuss for a long, long time.

"I'll hold you to that," she told him, giving him a blinding smile. "Are we talking wedding anniversaries here?"

Matt scowled. "What else?"

She shrugged and raised her brows. "I don't know. Usually when a man wants a woman to—"

His kiss stopped her teasing words. When he lifted his head they were both breathless. "You have to marry me."

"You're right." She brushed back his hair with gentle fingers. "I have to marry you." Smiling again, she said, "When?"

"Tomorrow. We'll drive across the border and—"

Libby shook her head. "Stop right there. No way am I going across any border. This is my first and last wedding, and I'm going to do it right. I want a white dress, Carla as maid of honor, my family around me, the whole works. We can have the ceremony and reception here in the yard if you like."

"How long will all this take?" Matt asked with a groan.

Libby squinted her eyes thoughtfully. "If we turn Carla loose on it, we can be married by the end of the month, if you like."

"I like," he told her with a quick grin. "Very much. As long as I don't have to move out until then."

"No moving," she promised. "We stay together. From now on."

Matt stood up and lifted her into his arms. "From now on," he agreed, heading inside the house. "Libby?"

"Umm?" She nestled closer, smiling when his heart pounded against her cheek.

"Do you think Eli will give us one of the whiz kids for a wedding present?"

*   *   *   *   *

SILHOUETTE

Desire

COMING NEXT MONTH

THE BEAUTY, THE BEAST AND THE BABY
Dixie Browning

Man of the Month and the second book in *Tall, Dark and Handsome*
Gorgeous Gus Wydowski couldn't change a baby's nappy to save his life, but
he also couldn't stay away from beautiful Mariah Brady. Mariah and her baby
were a package deal, so could Mariah turn the brooding bachelor into a family
man?

JUST A MEMORY AWAY Helen R. Myers

Francesca Jones couldn't believe it when she met a naked stranger suffering
from amnesia! She took him in and offered him her heart, and although he
instinctively responded to Frankie's satin skin and gentle hands, what could he
offer when he didn't even know his real name?

THE LAST GROOM ON EARTH Kristin James

So what if everyone thought Bryce Richards would make the perfect husband?
Angela Hewitt had fought enough childhood battles with him to know better.
But then he came to her rescue, and she began dreaming of forever with the last
man she'd marry!

ZOE AND THE BEST MAN Carole Buck

Wedding Belles
Zoe Armitage was on the lookout for her perfect husband. He had to be stable,
sincere...*nothing* like thrill-seeking, smooth-talking Gabriel Flynn. They'd
shared steamy kisses at their best friends' wedding, but that was just a romantic
game...

RIDGE: THE AVENGER Leanne Banks

Sons and Lovers
Ridge Jackson's plan was simple: protect Dara Seabrook and get revenge on
her godfather at the same time. Ridge was a professional; he knew the dangers
of mixing business with pleasure. How then had the voluptuous brunette got
under his skin?

SUTTON'S WAY Diana Palmer

Texan Lovers
Tragedy had sent Amanda Callaway to the Wyoming mountains to heal, but she
found another battle to fight...Quinn Sutton. Quinn didn't realize how special
his world seemed to Amanda, and she was determined to prove she shared the
same old-fashioned values—and desires. But when he learned who she was,
would she lose him forever?

COMING NEXT MONTH FROM
▼™ SILHOUETTE®

Sensation
A thrilling mix of passion, adventure and drama

THE RETURN OF EDEN McCALL Judith Duncan
OUR CHILD? Sally Tyler Hayes
THE COWBOY AND THE COSSACK
Merline Lovelace
THE HEART OF DEVIN MACKADE Nora Roberts

Intrigue
Danger, deception and desire

CRIME OF PASSION Maggie Ferguson
A KILLER SMILE Laura Kenner
THE VAGABOND Alexandra Sellers
MIDNIGHT KISS Rebecca York

Special Edition
Satisfying romances packed with emotion

SISTERS Penny Richards
TOO MANY MUMS Cathy Gillen Thacker
BUCHANAN'S BABY Pamela Toth
FOR LOVE OF HER CHILD Tracy Sinclair
THE REFORMER Diana Whitney
PLAYING DADDY Lorraine Carroll

One to Another

A year's supply of Silhouette Desire® novels— absolutely FREE!

Would you like to win a year's supply of seductive and breathtaking romances? Well, you can and they're FREE! Simply complete the missing word competition below and send it to us by 31st January 1997. The first 5 correct entries picked after the closing date will win a year's supply of Silhouette Desire novels (six books every month—worth over £160). What could be easier?

PAPER	B A C K	WARDS
ARM		MAN
PAIN		ON
SHOE		TOP
FIRE		MAT
WAIST		HANGER
BED		BOX
BACK		AGE
RAIN		FALL
CHOPPING		ROOM

Please turn over for details of how to enter ☞

How to enter...

There are ten missing words in our grid overleaf. Each of the missing words must connect up with the words on either side to make a new word—e.g. PAPER-BACK-WARDS. As you find each one, write it in the space provided, we've done the first one for you!

When you have found all the words, don't forget to fill in your name and address in the space provided below and pop this page into an envelope (you don't even need a stamp) and post it today. Hurry—competition ends 31st January 1997.

Silhouette® One to Another
FREEPOST
Croydon
Surrey
CR9 3WZ

Are you a Reader Service Subscriber?   Yes ❏   No ❏

Ms/Mrs/Miss/Mr _____

Address _____

_____

_____ Postcode _____

One application per household.

You may be mailed with other offers from other reputable companies as a result of this application. If you would prefer not to receive such offers, please tick box.   ❏

C296
A